KATIE'S REDEMPTION

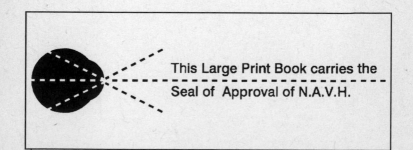

This Large Print Book carries the
Seal of Approval of N.A.V.H.

BRIDES OF AMISH COUNTRY

KATIE'S REDEMPTION

PATRICIA DAVIDS

THORNDIKE PRESS
A part of Gale, Cengage Learning

Detroit • New York • San Francisco • New Haven, Conn • Waterville, Maine • London

GALE
CENGAGE Learning

LIBRARY OF CONGRESS CATALOGING-IN-PUBLICATION DATA

Davids, Patricia.
   Katie's redemption / by Patricia Davids. — Large print ed.
     p. cm. — (Thorndike Press large print Christian romance)
   "Brides of Amish Country #1."
   ISBN-13: 978-1-4104-3187-5
   ISBN-10: 1-4104-3187-8
   1. Amish—Fiction. 2. Single mothers—Fiction. 3. Large type
books. I. Title.
PS3604.A9454K38 2010
813'.6—dc22   2010031541

Published in 2010 by arrangement with Harlequin Books S.A.

Even the sparrow has found a home,
and the swallow a nest for herself,
where she may have her young —
a place near your altar, O Lord Almighty,
my King and my God.

— *Psalms* 84:3

This book is dedicated to my family.
You have supported me every
step of the way
and I couldn't do it without you.

CHAPTER ONE

"Lady, you sure this is where you wanna get out?" The middle-aged bus driver tipped his hat back and regarded his passenger with worry-filled eyes.

"This is the place." Katie Lantz glanced from his concerned face to the desolate winter landscape beyond the windshield. A chill that owed nothing to the weather crawled over her skin.

It was her destination, but rural Ohio was the last place in the world she wanted to be. She had agonized over her decision for weeks. Now that she was here, the same worries that had robbed her of sleep for endless nights cartwheeled through her mind.

Would her brother take her in? What if Malachi turned her away? What would she do then? If he did allow her to return to his home would she ever find the strength to leave again?

"It don't feel right leaving a gal in your condition out here alone. You sure I can't take ya into town?"

"I'm sure." She pressed a protective hand to her midsection. Her condition was the only reason she was here. She didn't want to get off the bus, but what choice did she have?

None.

All her plans, her dreams and her hopes had turned to ashes. She took a deep breath and straightened her shoulders. "I'd just have to walk back if I went into Hope Springs. Thank you for letting me off. I know you aren't supposed to make unscheduled stops."

The driver pulled the lever to open the doors with obvious reluctance. "I don't make a habit of it, but I figured it was best not to argue with a gal that's as pregnant as you are."

A gust of wintry wind swirled in, raking Katie's face with icy fingers. A tremor raced through her body. She turned up the collar of her red plaid coat, prolonging the moment she would have to actually step out of the bus and back into the life she dreaded.

The driver seemed to sense her unwillingness to leave. "Is someone meeting you?"

She hadn't bothered to write that she was

coming. Her previous letters had all been returned unopened. Proof, if she needed any, that her family hadn't forgiven her for turning her back on her Amish heritage.

She lifted her chin.

I don't have to do this. I can stay on the bus and go to the next town.

And then what?

As quickly as her bravado appeared it evaporated. She closed her eyes. Her shoulders slumped in defeat.

All she had in her pocket was twelve dollars. All she owned was in the suitcase she clutched. It wasn't enough, not with her baby due in three weeks. For her child's sake, returning home was her only option.

For now.

Clinging to that faint echo of resolve, she drew a steadying breath, opened her eyes and faced her bleak future. "My brother's farm is just over the hill. It's not far. I'll be fine."

Oh, how she hoped her words would prove true.

She didn't belong in this Amish world. She had escaped it once before. She would do so again. It would be harder with a baby, but she would find a way.

With no money, without even a driver's license and nothing but an eighth-grade education, the English world was a hard place for an ex-Amish woman on her own.

Matt had taken her away and promised to take care of her and show her the wonders of the modern world, but his promises had been empty. He'd disappeared from her life three months ago, leaving her to struggle and fail alone.

The bus driver shrugged. "All right. You be careful."

"*Danki.* I mean . . . thank you." When she was upset the language of her childhood often slipped out. It was hard to remember to speak English when the words of her native Pennsylvania Dutch came to mind first.

Gripping her small case tightly, Katie descended the steps and walked toward the edge of the roadway. The doors slammed shut behind her. The engine roared as the driver pulled away, followed by a billowing cloud of diesel fumes.

There was no turning back — nowhere left to run.

Shivering as the frigid air found its way inside the coat she couldn't button over her bulging stomach, she pulled at the material to close the gap. Now she was truly alone. Except for the child she carried.

Standing here wasn't helping. She needed to get moving. Switching her suitcase to her other hand, she arched her back to stretch out a persistent cramp. When it eased, she turned and glanced up the long lane leading over the hill. For her baby she would do anything. Endure anything.

With the late-March sky hanging low and gray overhead, Katie wished for the first time that she had kept some of her Amish clothing. If she at least looked the part of a repentant Plain woman, her family reunion might go better.

She had left before her baptism — before taking her vows to faithfully follow the Plain faith. She would be reprimanded for her errant behavior, but she might not be shunned if she came asking forgiveness.

Please, God, don't let them send me away.

To give her child a home she would endure the angry tirade she expected from her brother. His wife, Beatrice, wouldn't intercede for Katie. Beatrice would sit silent and sullen, never saying a word. Through it all Malachi wouldn't be able to hide the gloating in his voice. He had predicted Katie would come to a bad end out among the English.

How she hated that he had been right.

Still, she would soon have the one thing her brother and her sister-in-law had been denied in their lives — a baby. Was it possible the arrival of her child might heal old wounds? Or would it only make things worse?

An unexpected tightening across her stomach made her draw in a quick breath. She had been up since dawn, riding for hours on the jolting bus. It was no wonder her back ached almost constantly now. She started toward the lane that led north from the highway. There could be no rest until she reached her brother's house.

The dirt road running between twin fences made for rough and treacherous walking. Buggy wheels and horse's hooves had cut deep ruts in the mud that was now frozen. Tiny, hard flakes driven by the wind stung her cheeks and made it difficult to see. She shivered and hunched deeper into her too-small coat.

As much as she wanted to hurry toward the warm stove she knew was glowing in her brother's kitchen, she couldn't. She had to be careful of each step over the rough ground. The last thing she wanted to do was fall and hurt the child that meant everything to her. When her son or daughter arrived, Katie would have the one true thing she had always longed for — a family of her own.

Her stomach tightened again. She had to stop to catch her breath. Her pain deepened.

14

Something wasn't right. This was more than fatigue. Had her long day of travel hurt the baby? She'd never forgive herself if something happened to her child.

After a few quick, panting breaths the discomfort passed. Katie straightened with relief. She switched her suitcase to her other hand, pushed her frozen fingers deep into her pocket and started walking again. She hadn't gone more than a hundred yards when the next pain made her double over and drop her case.

Fear clogged her throat as she clutched her belly. Breathing hard, she peered through the blowing snow. She could just make out the light from a window up ahead. It wasn't much farther. Closing her eyes, she gathered her strength.

One foot in front of the other. The only way to finish a journey is to start it.

With grim determination, she pressed on. Another dozen yards brought her to the steps of the small front porch. She sagged with relief when her hand closed over the railing. She was home.

Home. The word echoed inside her mind, bringing with it grim memories from the past. Defeat weighed down her already-low spirits. She raised her fist and knocked at the front door. Then she bowed her head

15

and closed her eyes, grasping the collar of her coat to keep the chill at bay.

When the door finally opened she looked up slowly past the dark trousers and suspenders, past the expanse of pale blue shirt to meet her brother's gaze.

Katie sucked in a breath and took a half step back. A tall, broad-shouldered Amish man stood in front of her with a kerosene lamp in his hand and a faint puzzled expression on his handsome face.

It wasn't Malachi.

Elam Sutter stared in surprise at the English woman on his doorstep clutching a suitcase in one hand and the collar of her coat with the other. Her pale face was framed by coal-black hair that ended just below her jawline. The way the ends of it swung forward to caress her cheeks reminded Elam of the wings of a small bird.

In his lamplight, snowflakes sparkled in her hair and on the tips of her thick eyelashes. Her eyes, dark as the night, brimmed with misery. She looked nearly frozen from her head . . . to her very pregnant belly.

He drew back in shock and raised the lamp higher, scanning the yard behind her for a car, but saw none. Perhaps it had broken down on the highway. That would

16

explain her sudden appearance.

The English! They hadn't enough sense to stay by a warm fire on such a fierce night. Still, she was obviously in trouble. He asked politely, "Can I help you?"

"Would you . . ." Her voice faltered. She swallowed hard then began again. "I must speak with Malachi."

"Would you be meaning Malachi Lantz?"

She pressed her lips together and nodded.

"The Lantz family doesn't live here anymore."

Her eyes widened in disbelief. "What? But this is his home."

"*Jah,* it was. He and his wife moved to Kansas last spring after he sold the farm to me. I have his address inside if you need it."

"That can't be," she whispered as she pressed a hand to her forehead.

"Who is it, Elam?" his mother, Nettie, called from behind him.

He spoke over his shoulder, "Someone looking for Malachi Lantz."

A second later his mother was beside him. She looked as shocked as he at the sight of a very pregnant outsider on their stoop, but it took only an instant for her kindheartedness to assert itself.

"Goodness, child, come in out of this terrible weather. You look chilled to the bone.

17

Elam, pull a chair close to the fireplace." She nudged him aside and he hurried to do as she instructed.

Grasping the woman's elbow, Nettie guided her guest into the living room and helped her into a straight-backed seat, one of a pair that flanked the stone fireplace.

"*Ach,* your hands are like ice." Nettie began rubbing them between her own.

The young woman's gaze roved around the room and finally came to rest on Elam's mother's face. "Malachi doesn't live here anymore?"

Nettie's gaze softened. "No, dear. I'm sorry. He moved away."

Pulling her hands away from the older woman's, she raked them through her dark hair. "Why would he move? Was it because of me?"

Elam exchanged puzzled glances with his mother. What did the woman mean by that comment? Nettie shrugged, then took the girl's hands once more. "What's your name, child?"

The dazed look on his visitor's face was replaced by a blankness that troubled him. "My name is Katie."

"Katie, I'm Nettie Sutter, and this is my son, Elam."

Katie bent forward with a deep moan. "I

don't know what to do."

"Don't cry." His mother patted the girl's shoulder as she shot Elam a worried glance.

After several deep breaths, Katie straightened and wiped her cheeks. "I have to go."

"You haven't thawed out yet. At least stay for a cup of tea. The kettle is still on. Elam, bring me a cup, too." Nettie caught his eye and made shooing motions toward the kitchen with one hand.

He retreated, but he could still hear them talking as he fixed the requested drinks. His mother's tone was calm and reassuring as she said, "Why not stay and rest a bit longer? It's not good for your baby to have his mother turning into an icicle."

"I need to go. I have to find Malachi." Katie's voice wavered with uncertainty.

"Is he the father?" Nettie asked gently.

Elam didn't want to think ill of any man, but why else would a pregnant woman show up demanding to see Malachi months after he had moved away?

"No. He's my brother."

Elam stopped pouring the hot water and glanced toward the living room. He had heard the story of Malachi's willful sister from the man's own lips. So this was the woman that had left the Amish after bringing shame to her family. At least she had done so before her baptism.

Elam placed the tea bags in the mugs. Malachi had his sympathy. Elam knew what it was like to face such heartbreak — the talk, the pitying looks, the whispers behind a man's back.

He pushed aside those memories as he carried the cups into the other room. "I didn't see your car outside."

She looked up at him and once again the sadness in her luminous eyes caught him like a physical blow. Her lower lip quivered. "I came on the bus."

Elam felt his mother's eyes on him but he kept his gaze averted, focusing instead on handing over the hot drinks without spilling any.

Nettie took a cup from Elam and pressed it into Katie's hands. "Have a sip. This will warm you right up. You can't walk all the way to Hope Springs tonight. Elam will take you in the buggy when you're ready."

Katie shook her head. "I can't ask you to do that."

"It's no trouble." He tried hard to mean it. He'd already finished a long day of work and he was ready for his bed. He would have to be up again before dawn to milk the cows and feed the livestock.

Returning to the kitchen, he began donning his coat and his black felt hat. It was a mean night for a ride into town, but what else could he do? He certainly couldn't let her walk, in her condition.

Suddenly, he heard Katie cry out. Rushing back into the room, he saw her doubled over, the mug lying broken on the floor in a puddle at her feet.

CHAPTER TWO

Through a haze of pain, Katie heard Elam ask, "What is it? What's wrong?"

She felt strong arms supporting her. She leaned into his strength but she couldn't answer because she was gritting her teeth to keep from screaming.

"I believe her baby's coming," Nettie replied calmly.

Panic swallowed Katie whole.

This can't be happening. Not here. Not with strangers. This isn't right. Nothing is right. Please, God, I know I've disappointed You, but help me now.

A horrible sensation settled in the pit of her stomach. Was this her punishment for leaving the faith? She knew there would be a price to pay someday, but she didn't want her baby to suffer because of her actions.

She looked from Elam's wide, startled eyes above her to his mother's serene face. "My baby can't come now. I'm not due for three weeks."

Nettie's smile was reassuring. "Babies have a way of choosing their own time."

Katie bit her lower lip to stop its trembling. She'd never been so scared in all her life.

"Don't worry. I know just what to do. I've had eight of my own." Nettie's unruffled demeanor eased some of Katie's panic. Seeing no other choice, Katie allowed Nettie to take charge of the situation.

Why wasn't Matt here when she needed him? It should have been Matt beside her, not these people.

Because he'd grown tired of her, that's why. He had been ashamed of her backward ways. Her pregnancy had been the last straw. He accused her of getting pregnant to force him into marriage, which wasn't true. After their last fight three months ago, he walked out and never came back, leaving her with rent and bills she couldn't pay.

Nettie turned to her son. "Elam, move one of the extra beds into the kitchen so Katie has a warm place to rest while you fetch the midwife."

"Jah." A blush of embarrassment stained his cheeks dark red. His lack of a beard proclaimed his single status. Childbirth was the territory of women, clearly a territory

he didn't want to explore. He hurried away.

Nettie coaxed Katie to sit and showed her how to breathe through her next contraction. When Elam had wrestled a narrow bed into the kitchen and piled several quilts on one end, Nettie helped Katie onto it. Lying down with a sigh of relief, Katie closed her eyes. She was so tired. "I can't do this."

"Yes, you can. The Lord will give you the strength you need," Nettie said gently.

No, He won't. God doesn't care what happens to a sinner like me.

"Is the midwife okay, or will you be wanting to go to a hospital?" Elam's voice interrupted her fatalistic thoughts.

She turned her face toward the wall. "I can't afford a hospital."

"The midwife will do fine, Elam. I've heard good things about Nurse Bradley from the women hereabouts. Go over to the Zimmerman farm and ask to use their phone. They'll know her number. What are you waiting for? Get a move on."

"I was wondering if there was anyone else I should call. Perhaps the baby's father? He should know his child is being born."

"Matt doesn't care about this baby. He left us," Katie managed to say through gritted teeth. The growing contraction required all her concentration. The slamming of the

24

outside door signaled that Elam had gone.

When her pain eased, Katie turned back to watch Nettie bustling about, making preparations for her baby's arrival. The kitchen looked so different than it had during the years Katie had lived here. She could see all of the changes Elam and his mother had made. She concentrated on each detail as she tried to relax and gather strength for her next contraction.

Overhead, a new gas lamp above the kitchen table cast a warm glow throughout the room. As it had in her day, a rectangular table occupied the center of the room. The chairs around it were straight-backed and sturdy. The dark, small cabinets that once flanked the wide window above the sink had been replaced with new larger ones that spread across the length of the wall. Their natural golden oak color was much more appealing.

Setting Katie's suitcase on a chair, Nettie opened it and drew out a pink cotton nightgown. "Let's get you into something more comfortable."

Embarrassment sent the blood rushing to Katie's face, but Nettie didn't seem to notice. The look of kindness on her face and her soothing prattle in thick German quickly put Katie at ease. Elam's mother seemed perfectly willing to accept a stranger into her home and care for her.

Dressed in a dark blue dress covered by a black apron, Nettie had a sparkle in her eyes behind the wire-rimmed glasses perched on her nose. Her plump cheeks were creased with smile lines. No one in Katie's family had ever been cheerful.

Nettie's gray hair was parted in the middle and coiled into a bun beneath her white *kapp* the way all Amish women wore their hair. Katie fingered her own short locks.

Cutting her hair had been her first act of rebellion after she left home. Amish women never cut their hair. It had been one way Katie could prove to herself that she was no longer Amish. At times, she regretted the loss of her waist-length hair. She once thought she despised all things Amish, yet this Amish woman was showing her more kindness than anyone had ever done. Only one person Katie knew in the neighborhood where she'd lived with Matt would have taken her in like this, but that friend was dead. The English world wasn't always a friendly place.

After she had changed into her night-clothes, Katie settled back into bed. Nettie added more wood to the stove. The familiar crackle, hiss and popping sounds of the fire helped calm Katie's nerves. Until the next contraction hit.

Elam wasted no time getting Judy hitched to the buggy. In spite of her master's attempts to hurry, the black mare balked at the wide doorway, making it clear she objected to leaving her warm barn. Elam couldn't blame her. The windblown sleet felt like stinging nettles where it hit his face. He pulled the warm scarf his mother had knitted for him over his nose and mouth, then climbed inside the carriage.

The town of Hope Springs lay three miles to the east of his farm. He had Amish neighbors on all sides. None of them used telephones. The nearest phone was at the Zimmerman farm just over a mile away. He prayed the Mennonite family would be at home when he got there or he would have to go all the way into town to find one.

Once he reached the highway, he urged Judy to pick up her pace. He slapped the reins against her rump and frequently checked the rectangular mirror mounted on the side of his buggy. This stretch of curving road could be a nerve-racking drive in daylight. Traveling it in this kind of weather was doubly dangerous. The English cars and trucks came speeding by with little regard

27

for the fact that a slow-moving buggy might be just over the rise.

Tonight, as always, Elam trusted the Lord to see him safely to his destination, but he kept a sharp lookout for headlights coming up behind him.

It was a relief to finally swing off the blacktop onto the gravel drive of his neighbor's farm. By the time he reached their yard, his scarf was coated with ice from his frozen breath. He saw at once that the lights were on. The Zimmermans were home. He gave a quick prayer of thanks.

Hitching Judy to the picket fence near the front gate, he bounded up the porch steps. Pulling down his muffler, he rapped on the door.

Grace Zimmerman answered his knock. "Elam, what on earth are you doing out on a night like this?"

He nodded to her. "*Goot* evening, Mrs. Zimmerman. I've come to ask if I might use your telephone, please."

"Of course. Is something wrong? Is your mother ill?"

"*Mamm* is fine. We've a visitor, a young woman who's gone into labor."

"Shall I call 911 and get an ambulance?"

"*Mamm* says the midwife will do."

"Okay. Come in and I'll get that number

for you."

"My thanks."

The midwife answered on the second ring. "Nurse Bradley speaking."

"Miss Bradley, I am Elam Sutter, and I have need of your services."

"Babies never check the weather report before they decide to make an appearance, do they? Has your wife been into the clinic before?"

"It is not my wife. It is a woman who is visiting in the area, so she hasn't been to see you."

"Oh. Okay, give me the patient's name."

He knew Katie's maiden name, but he didn't know her married name. Was the man she spoke of her husband? Deciding it didn't matter, he said, "Her name is Katie Lantz."

"Is Mrs. Lantz full term?"

"I'm not sure."

"How far apart are her contractions? Is it her first baby?"

"That I don't know. My mother is with her and she said to call you," he stated firmly. He was embarrassed at not being able to answer her questions

"Are there complications?"

"Not that I know of, but you would be the best judge of that."

"All right. How do I find your place?"

He gave her directions. She repeated them, then cheerfully assured him that she would get there as fast as she could.

As he hung up the phone, Mrs. Zimmerman withdrew a steaming cup from her microwave. "Have a cup of hot cocoa before you head back into the storm, Elam. Did I hear you say that Katie Lantz is having a baby?"

"*Jah.* She came looking for her brother. She didn't know he had moved." He took the cup and sipped it gratefully, letting the steam warm his face. Mrs. Zimmerman was a kindhearted woman but she did love to gossip.

"Poor Katie. Is Matt with her?" She seemed genuinely distressed.

"She's alone. Is Matt her husband? Do you know how to contact him?"

Mrs. Zimmerman shook her head. "I have no idea if they married. Matt Carson was a friend of my grandson's from college. The boys spent a few weeks here two summers ago. That's how Katie met Matt. I'll call William and see if he has kept in touch with Matt or his family."

"Thank you."

"I never thought Katie would come back. Malachi was furious at the attention Matt

30

paid her. If he hadn't overreacted I think the romance would have died a natural death when Matt went back to school. I don't normally speak ill of people, but Malachi was very hard on that girl, even when she was little."

" 'Train up a child in the way he should go: and when he is old, he will not depart from it.' *Proverbs* 22:6," Elam quoted.

"I agree the tree grows the way the sapling is bent, but not if it's snapped in half. I even spoke to Bishop Zook about Malachi's treatment of Katie when she was about ten but I don't think it did any good. I wasn't all that surprised when she ran off with Matt."

Elam didn't feel right gossiping about Katie or her family. He took another sip of the chocolate, then set the cup on the counter. "*Danki,* Mrs. Zimmerman. I'd best be getting back."

"I'll keep Katie in my prayers. Please tell her I said hello."

"I will, and thank you again." He wrapped his scarf around his face and headed out the door.

By the time Elam returned home, the midwife had already arrived. Her blue station wagon sat in front of the house collecting a coating of snow on the hood and

31

windshield.

He lit a lantern and hung it inside the barn so his mother would know he was back if she looked out. He took his time making sure Judy was rubbed down and dry before returning her to her stall with an extra ration of oats for her hard work. When he was done, he stood facing the house from the wide barn door. The snow was letting up and the wind was dying down at last.

Lamplight glowed from the kitchen window and he wondered how Katie was faring. He couldn't imagine finding himself cast upon the mercy of strangers at such a time. He had seven brothers and sisters plus cousins galore that he could turn to at a moment's notice for help. It seemed that poor Katie had no one.

Knowing his presence wouldn't be needed or wanted in the house, he decided he might as well get some work done if he wasn't going to get any sleep. Taking the lantern down, he carried it to the workshop he'd set up inside the barn. Once there, he lit the gas lamps hanging overhead. They filled the space with light. He turned out the portable lamp and set it on the counter.

The tools of his carpentry and wooden basket–making business were hung neatly on the walls. Everything was in order —

exactly the way he liked it. Along, narrow table sat near the windows with five chairs along its length. Several dozen baskets in assorted sizes and shapes were stacked in bins against the far wall. Cedar, poplar and pine boards on sawhorses filled the air with their fresh, woody scents.

Only a year ago the room had been a small feed storage area, but as the demand for his baskets and woodworking expanded, he'd needed more space. Remodeling the workshop had been his winter project and it was almost done. The clean white walls were meant to reflect the light coming in from the extra windows he'd added. When summer took hold of the land, the windows would open to let in the cool breezes. It was a good shop, and he was pleased with what he'd accomplished.

Stoking the coals glowing in a small stove, he soon had a bright fire burning. It wasn't long before the chill was gone from the air. He took off his coat and hung it on a peg near the frost-covered windows. Using his sleeve, he rubbed one windowpane clear so he could see the house.

Light flooded from the kitchen window. They must have moved more lamps into the room. Knowing he couldn't help, he pick up his measuring tape and began marking sections of cedar board for a hope chest a client had ordered last week.

He didn't need to concentrate on the task. His hands knew the wood, knew the tools he held as if they were extensions of his own fingers. His gaze was drawn repeatedly to the window and the drama he knew was being played out inside his home. As he worked, he prayed for Katie Lantz and her unborn child.

Hours later, he glanced out the window and stopped his work abruptly. He saw his mother hurrying toward him. Had something gone wrong?

CHAPTER THREE

"You are so beautiful," Katie whispered. Tears blurred her vision and she rapidly blinked them away.

Propped up with pillows against the headboard of her borrowed bed, she drew her fingers gently across the face of her daughter where she lay nestled in the crook of her arm. Her little head was covered in dark hair. Her eyelashes lay like tiny curved spikes against her cheeks. She was the most beautiful thing Katie had ever seen.

Amber Bradley, the midwife, moved about the other side of the room, quietly putting her things away. Katie had been a little surprised that the midwife wasn't Amish. That the women of the district trusted an outsider spoke volumes for Amber. She was both kind and competent, as Katie had discovered.

When Amber came over to the bed at last, she sat gently on the edge and asked, "Shall

I take her now? You really do need some rest."

"Can I hold her just a little longer?" Katie didn't want to give her baby over to anyone. Not yet. The joy of holding her own child was too new, too wonderful to allow it to end.

Amber smiled and nodded. "All right, but I do need to check her over more completely before I go. We didn't have a lot of time to discuss your plans. Maybe we can do that now."

Reality poked its ugly head back into Katie's mind. Her plans hadn't changed. They had simply been delayed. "I intend to go to my brother's house."

"Does he live close by?"

"No. Mr. Sutter said Malachi has moved to Kansas."

"I see. That's a long way to travel with a newborn."

Especially for someone who had no money. And now she owed the midwife, as well. All Katie could do was be honest with Amber. She glanced up at the nurse. "I'm grateful you came tonight, but I'm sorry I can't pay you right now. I will, I promise. As soon as I get a job."

"I'm not worried about that. The Amish always pay their bills. In fact, they're much more prompt than any insurance company I've dealt with."

Katie looked down at her daughter. "I'm not Amish. Not anymore."

"Don't be worrying about my fee. Just enjoy that beautiful baby. I'll send a bill in a few days and you can pay me when you're able."

The outside door opened and Nettie rushed in carrying a large, oval wooden basket. She was followed by Elam. He paused long enough to hang his coat and hat by the door, then he approached the bed. "I heard it's a fine, healthy girl. Congratulations, Katie Lantz."

"Thank you." She proudly pulled back the corner of the receiving blanket, a gift from Amber, to show Elam her little girl.

He moved closer and leaned down, but kept his hands tucked in the front pockets of his pants. *"Ach,* she's *wundascheen!"*

"Thank you. I think she's beautiful, too." Katie planted a kiss on her daughter's head.

Nettie set the basket on the table, folded her arms over her ample chest and grinned. *"Jah,* she looks like her Mama with all that black hair."

Reaching out hesitantly, Elam touched the baby's tiny fist. "Have you given her a name?"

"Rachel Ann. It was my mother's name."

Nodding his satisfaction, he straightened and shoved his hand back in his pocket. "It's a *goot* name. A plain name."

Katie blinked back sudden tears as she gazed at her daughter. Even though they would have to live with Malachi for a while, Rachel would not be raised Amish as Katie's mother had been. Why did that make her feel sad?

Amber rose from her place at the foot of the bed. "I see you've got a solution for where this little one is going to sleep, Nettie."

"My daughter, Mary, is expecting in a few months. She has my old cradle, but a folded quilt will make this a comfortable bed for Rachel. What do you think, Katie?"

"I think it will do fine." All of the sudden, Katie was so tired she could barely keep her eyes open.

"I will make a bassinet for her," Elam offered quickly. "It won't take any time at all."

Overwhelmed, Katie said, "You've been so kind already, Mr. Sutter. How can I ever thank you?"

"Someday, you will do a kindness for someone in need. That will be my thanks," he replied, soft and low so that only she could hear him.

Katie studied his face in the lamplight. It was the first time she had really looked at him. He was probably twenty-five years old. Most Amish men his age were married with one or two children already. She wondered why he was still single. He was certainly handsome enough to please any young woman. His hair, sable-brown and thick, held a touch of unruly curl where it brushed the back of his collar.

His face, unlike his hair, was all chiseled angles and planes, from his broad forehead to his high cheekbones. That, coupled with a straight, no-nonsense nose, gave him a look of harshness. Until she noticed his eyes. Soft sky-blue eyes that crinkled at the corners when he smiled as he was smiling now at the sight of Rachel's pink bow mouth opened in a wide yawn.

"Looks like someone is ready to try out her new bed." He stepped back as Amber came to take Rachel from Katie.

"I know her mother could use some rest," Amber stated with a stern glance in Katie's direction.

Katie nodded in agreement, but she didn't want to sleep. "If I close my eyes for a few minutes, that's all I need."

"You're going to need much more than that," Nettie declared, placing the quilt-lined basket on a kitchen chair beside Katie's bed.

Amber laid the baby on the table and unwrapped her enough to listen to her heart and lungs with a stethoscope. Katie couldn't close her eyes until she knew all was well. After finishing her examination, Amber rewrapped the baby tightly and laid her in the basket. "Everything looks good, but I'll be back to check on her tomorrow, and you, too, Mommy. I'll also draw a little blood from her heel tomorrow. The state requires certain tests on all newborns. You'll get the results in a few weeks. I can tell you're tired, Katie. We'll talk about it tomorrow."

Katie scooted down under the covers and rolled to her side so that she could see her daughter. "Will she be warm enough?"

"She'll be fine. We'll keep the stove going all night," Nettie promised.

"She's so sweet. I can't believe how much I love her already." Sleep pulled Katie's eyelids lower. She fought it, afraid if she slept she would wake and find it all had been a dream.

The murmur of voices reached her. She heard her name mentioned and struggled to understand what was being said.

"I'm worried about Katie." It was Amber talking.

"Why?" came Elam's deep voice.

Opening her eyes, Katie saw that everyone had gone into the living room. She strained to hear them.

Amber said, "It's clear she hasn't been eating well for some time. Plus, her blood loss was heavier than I like to see. Physically, she's very run-down."

"Do you think she should go to the hospital?" Elam asked. Katie heard the worry behind his words.

He was concerned about her. She smiled at the thought. It had been a long time since anyone had worried about her. As hard as she tried, she couldn't keep her eyes open any longer.

Concerned for his unexpected guest's health, Elam glanced from the kitchen door to the nurse standing beside his mother.

Amber shook her head. "I don't think she needs to go to the hospital, but I do think she should take it easy for a few days. She needs good hearty food, lots of rest and plenty of fluids. I understand she was on her way to her brother's home?"

"*Jah,*" Nettie said. "When she realized he wasn't here, she said she was going to the bus station."

Amber scowled and crossed her arms.

41

"She shouldn't travel for a while. Not for at least a week, maybe two. If having her here is an inconvenience, I can try to make other arrangements in town until her family can send someone for her."

Elam could see his mother struggling to hold back her opinion. He was the man of the house. It would have to be his decision.

At least that was the way it was supposed to work, but he had learned a valuable lesson about women from his father. His *dat* used to say, "Women get their way by one means or another, son. Make a woman mad only if you're willing to eat burnt bread until she decides otherwise. The man who tells you he's in charge in his own house will lie about other things, too."

His father had been wise about so many things and yet so foolish in the end.

Elam's mother might want Katie to remain with them, but Elam was hesitant about the idea. The last thing he needed was to stir up trouble in his new church district. Katie wasn't a member of his family. She had turned her back on her Amish upbringing. Her presence might even prompt unwanted gossip. His family had endured enough of that.

"I certainly wouldn't mind having another woman in the house." It seemed his mother

42

couldn't be silent for long.

This wasn't a discussion he wanted to have in front of an outsider. He said, "Nothing can be done tonight. We'll talk it over with Katie in the morning."

The faint smile that played across Nettie's lips told him she'd already made up her mind. "The woman needs help. It's our Christian duty to care for her and that precious baby."

Mustering a stern tone, he said, "You don't fool me, *Mamm.* I saw how excited you were to tell me it was a little girl. The way you came running out to the barn, I thought the house must be on fire. You're just happy to have a new baby in the house. I've heard you telling your friends that you're hoping Mary's next one is a girl."

His mother raised one finger toward the ceiling. "*Gott* has given me five fine grandsons. I'm not complaining. I pray only that my daughters have more healthy children. If one or two should be girls — that is *Gotte wille,* too, and fine with me. Just as it was *Gotte wille* that Katie and her baby came to us."

Her logic was something Elam couldn't argue with. He turned to the nurse. "She can stay here until her family comes to fetch her if that is what she wants. She can write to Malachi in the morning and tell him that she's here."

Amber looked relieved. "Wonderful. That's settled, then."

For Malachi's sake and for Katie's, Elam prayed that she was prepared to mend her ways and come back to the Amish. If she was sincere about returning, the church members would welcome her back with open arms.

Amber gathered up her bag. "I'll come by late tomorrow afternoon to check on both of my patients. I'm going to leave some powdered infant formula with you in case the nursing doesn't go well, but I'm sure you won't need it. Please don't hesitate to send for me if you think something is wrong. Mrs. Sutter, I'm sure you know what to look for."

"Thank you for coming, Miss Bradley."

"Thank you for calling me."

Elam hesitated, then said, "About your bill."

She waved his concern aside. "Katie and I have already discussed it."

After she left, a calm settled over the house. Nettie tried to hide a yawn, but Elam saw it. The clock on the wall said it was nearly two in the morning. At least it was the off Sunday and they would not have to travel to services in the morning. "Go to bed, *Mamm*."

"No, I'm going to sleep here in my chair in case Katie or the baby needs me."

He knew better than to argue with her. "I'll get a quilt and a pillow from your room."

"Thank you, Elam. You are a good son."

A few minutes later he returned with the bedding and handed it to her. As she settled herself in her favorite brown wingback chair, he moved a footstool in front of it and helped her prop up her feet, then tucked the blanket under them. She sighed heavily and set her glasses on the small, oval reading table beside her.

When he was sure she was comfortable, he quietly walked back into the kitchen. Before heading upstairs to his room, he checked the fire in the stove. It had died down to glowing red coals. The wood box beside it was almost empty. The women must have used most of it keeping the room warm for Katie's delivery. Glancing toward the bed in the corner, he watched Katie sleeping huddled beneath a blue-and-green patterned quilt.

She looked so small and alone.

Only she wasn't alone. Her baby slept on a chair beside the bed in one of his baskets.

And what of the child's father? Katie had said he didn't care about them, but what man would not care that he had such a beautiful daughter? There was a lot Elam didn't know about his surprise guest, but answers would have to wait until morning.

Quietly slipping into his coat, he eased the door open and went out to fetch more wood. He paused on the front steps to admire the view. A three-quarter moon sent its bright light across the farmyard, making the trees and buildings cast sharp black shadows over the snow. High in the night sky, the stars twinkled as if in competition with the sparkling landscape.

Elam shook his head. He was being fanciful again. It was a habit he tried hard to break. Still, it had to be good for a man to stop and admire the handiwork of God. Why else did he have eyes to see and ears to hear?

Elam's breath rose in the air in frosty puffs as he loaded his arms with wood and returned to the house. He managed to open the door with one hand, but it banged shut behind him. He froze, hoping he hadn't disturbed his guests or his mother. When no one moved, he blew out the breath he'd been holding and began unloading his burden as quietly as he could.

After adding a few of his logs to the stove, he stoked up the blaze and closed the firebox door. He had taken a half-dozen steps toward the stairs and the bed that was calling to him when the baby started to fuss. He spun around.

Katie stirred but didn't open her eyes. He could hear his mother's not-so-soft snoring in the other room. The baby quieted.

He took a step back and grimaced as the floorboard creaked. Immediately, the baby started her soft fussing again. Elam waited, but neither of the women woke. The baby's cries weren't loud. Maybe she was just lonely in a strange new place.

He crossed the room. Squatting beside the basket, he rocked it gently. The moonlight spilling in through the kitchen window showed him a tiny face with bright eyes wide open.

"Shh," he whispered as he rocked her. Rachel showed no inclination to go back to sleep. Her attempts to catch her tight fists in her mouth amused him. What a cute little pumpkin she was. Another of God's wonders.

Glancing once more at Katie's pale face, he picked the baby up. She immediately quieted. He crossed the room and sat down at the table. "Let's let your mama sleep a bit longer."

He disapproved of the choices this little one's mother had made, but none of that disapproval spilled over onto this new life. Settling her into the crook of his arm, he marveled at how tiny she was and yet how complete. The cares and worries of his day slipped away. A softness nestled itself around his heart. What would it be like to hold a child of his own? Would he ever know? Rachel yawned and he smiled at her.

"Ah, I was right. You just wanted someone to cuddle you. I know a thing or two about wee ones. You're not the first babe I've held."

Babies certainly weren't new to him. He'd rocked nephews aplenty. He raised her slightly to make her more comfortable.

"My sisters think nothing of plopping a babe in my arms so they're free to help *Mamm* with canning or gardening, but I know what they're up to," he whispered to the cute baby he held.

"They think if I'm reminded how wonderful children are I'll start going to the Sunday night singings again and court a wife of my own. They don't see that I'm not ready for that."

He wasn't sure he would ever be ready to trust his heart to someone again. If that time did come, it would only be with a woman he was certain shared his love of God and his Plain faith.

"Once burned, twice shy, as the English say," he confided to his tiny listener.

He waited for the anger to surface but it didn't. For the first time in over a year he was able to think about his broken engagement without bitterness. Maybe the sweet-smelling babe in his arms had brought with her a measure of God's peace for him. To her, life was new and good and shouldn't be tainted with the sins of the past.

He began to sing a soft lullaby in his native tongue. Rachel stared back at him intently for a few minutes, but she eventually grew discontent with his voice and the fingers she couldn't quite get in her mouth. Her little fussing noises became a full-fledged cry.

"I guess I can't fix what ails you after all. I reckon I'll have to wake your mother."

"I'm awake." Katie's low voice came from the bed.

He looked over to find her watching him with dark eyes as beautiful and intense as her daughter's. How long had she been listening to him?

CHAPTER FOUR

Katie met Elam's gaze across the room. Moonlight streaming through the windows cut long rectangles of light across the plank floor. It gave her enough light to see the way Elam held her daughter. With confidence, caring and gentleness. Would Matt have done the same? Somehow, she didn't think so.

Her boyfriend's charm had evaporated quickly, once the novelty of having an Amish girlfriend wore off. When he found himself stuck with a "stupid Amish bumpkin" who couldn't use a microwave and didn't know how to work a cell phone, he reverted to his true nature. The harder Katie tried to make him happy, the more resentful he became. The harder she tried to prove her love, the louder he complained that she was smothering him. Looking back, it seemed that their relationship had been doomed from the start.

Her elderly landlady back in Columbus once said, "Honey, that man's a case of bad judgment. Dump him before he dumps you."

Katie hadn't wanted to believe Mrs. Pearlman, but it turned out she knew what she was talking about.

Elam spoke as he rose to his feet, yanking Katie's attention back to the present. "I was trying to get Rachel to go back to sleep without waking you."

"The song you were singing, what's it called?"

"You don't know *In der Stillen Einsamkeit?*" He sounded genuinely surprised.

"No."

"I thought every Amish child had heard it. My mother sang it to all of us and still sings it to her grandchildren."

"There wasn't a lot of singing in my house. I don't remember my mother ever singing. I have very few clear memories of my family. My father died before I was born in some kind of farm accident. I do remember my brother Hans playing with me. He was always laughing. He gave me a doll that I loved, and he gave me piggyback rides. I remember someone scolding him to be careful. I think it was my mother."

"What happened to your family?"

"Everyone except Malachi and I died in a fire when I was four."

"I'm sorry."

Katie shrugged off his sympathy. "It was a long time ago."

Rachel gave another lusty cry. Elam said, "I think she's telling me I make a poor substitute for her mother."

Katie shifted into a sitting position in the bed and held out her arms. When Elam laid her daughter in her embrace, she said, "I'm afraid she's going to think I'm a poor substitute for a mother when she gets to know me."

"My sisters all worried that they wouldn't make good mothers, but they learned. You will, too."

"I hope you're right." He sounded so matter-of-fact. Like it was a done deal. She wanted to believe him, but she had made such a mess of her life up to this point.

"My mother will help as long as you're here. If you let her."

"I'm not sure I could stop her. She's something of a force of nature."

Chuckling softly, he nodded. *"Jah,* that is a good description of *Mamm."*

As their eyes met, Katie experienced a strange thrill, a sizzling connection with Elam that both surprised and delighted her.

Rachel quieted. Elam's expression changed. The amusement left his gaze, replaced by an odd intensity that sent heat rushing to Katie's cheeks.

Since the baby had quieted, Katie simply held and admired her. Stroking one of her daughter's sweetly curved brows, Katie said, "This wasn't the way I planned for you to come into the world."

Elam folded his arms. "Our best laid plans often come to naught."

"My landlady used to say, 'Man plans, God laughs.'" Katie tried to imitate her friend's broad Yiddish accent.

"She sounds like a wise woman."

Katie nodded sadly. "She was a very wise woman."

If Mrs. Pearlman had lived, Katie wouldn't be in this mess. Her kind landlady would have taken her in until she found a job. God had once again taken away the person who truly cared about her, leaving Katie where she had always been. Alone, unwanted, belonging nowhere.

She glanced up at Elam as he towered over her bed. "Your mother reminds me of my friend. She had the same kind eyes."

When he didn't say anything, Katie sighed. "I know what you're thinking."

Frowning slightly, he asked, "And what

would that be?"

"You're thinking I didn't plan very well at all."

He crossed his arms and looked at the floor. "I didn't say that."

"No, you didn't, but it's the truth. I kept thinking that Matt would come back for me. For us."

"How long ago did he leave you?"

"Three months. After that I got a part-time job working for our landlady, but she died and the place was sold. I waited for him to come back until my rent ran out. I only had enough money left to buy a bus ticket here."

"Your husband should not have left you."

It was her turn to look away. The shame she'd tried so hard to ignore left a bitter taste in her mouth. "Matt Carson wasn't my husband."

"Ah." It was all Elam said, but to her ears that one syllable carried a wealth of condemnation and pity.

After a long moment, he said, "You should know that Grace Zimmerman mentioned Matt was a friend of her grandson when I went there to use the phone. She said she would have her grandson try and contact Matt. Perhaps he will come for you when he finds out you are here."

Rachel began to fuss again. Katie bounced her gently. "Matt had plenty of time to come for us when we were in the city. I don't expect he will come now. We won't be a burden to you or your family any longer than necessary."

"We will not turn you out. That is not our way. The Bible commands us to help those in need."

"I'm grateful for all you've done, but I'll go on to my brother as soon as possible."

Nettie appeared in the living room doorway rubbing her neck. "There's no need to speak of traveling yet. The nurse says you're to rest. You can write to Malachi and tell him your situation, but you will stay here for a few days. Or more if you need it."

Katie bit her lip. Writing her brother would not be enough. She had to go to Malachi in person. He'd made that abundantly clear the day she left with Matt. His angry words still echoed inside her head.

"You ungrateful harlot, you've brought shame on me since the day you were born. You'll not last six months out in the English world. When you come to your senses you'll be back. But know this. You are dead to me until I see you kneeling in front of me and begging my forgiveness."

At the time, she felt only relief at getting

away from her brother's strict control. In the months that followed, when it became clear that running away with Matt had been a bad decision, Katie came to realize that she did still care about her brother and she was sorry for the way she'd left.

Matt laughed at her and called her spineless when she decided to try and mend things with her only sibling. She had written several long letters of apology, but each one came back unopened. After two months, she gave up trying. When Matt left she didn't bother writing to her brother. She knew he meant what he'd said.

Rachel started crying again. Nettie waved a hand to send Elam on his way. "We'll talk about this tomorrow. Right now this little one is hungry and she doesn't want to wait any longer."

Elam bid her good-night, then turned away and headed for the stairs leading to the upper story.

Katie was sorry their quiet talk had ended. She would have enjoyed spending more time with him.

As soon as the thought occurred, she chided herself for such feelings. The last thing she needed was to complicate her life with another man. She appreciated Elam's kindness, but she wouldn't mistake those feelings for anything more.

After that, all Katie's attention was taken up trying to satisfy her daughter's hungry demands. Later, as Katie fell asleep again, she dreamed about Elam rocking her baby in his arms and singing a soft lullaby. In her dream, the sound of his voice soothed her spirit and brought with it a quiet peacefulness.

For most of the next two days all Katie did was doze and feed the baby. Nettie took over the job of nursemaid, in addition to running her household, without missing a beat and with undisguised gentle joy. At her insistence, Katie was allowed to rest, drink plenty of hearty chicken soup, nurse her baby and nothing else.

Elam had moved a folding screen into the kitchen and placed it in front of her bed to give her and the baby some privacy, then he vanished for most of the day to do his chores and work in his woodshop.

Katie saw so little of him that she began to wonder if he was deliberately trying to avoid spending time with her. When he was in the house, she felt none of the closeness they'd shared the night Rachel was born. She began to think she'd simply imagined the connection they had shared.

The midwife returned as promised to check on Katie and the baby. Amber came bearing a gift of disposable diapers, several blankets and baby gowns which she insisted were donations made by the community for just such an occasion. While Rachel scored glowing marks and was pronounced as healthy as a horse, Amber wasn't quite as pleased with Katie's progress.

"At least another day of bed rest is in order. If your color and your blood pressure aren't better by tomorrow, I may send you to the hospital after all."

"I promise I will take it easy," Katie assured Amber. It was an easy promise to keep. Deep fatigue pulled at her limbs and made even the simplest task, like changing diapers, into an exhausting exercise.

"Mrs. Sutter will tell me if you aren't." Amber glanced at Nettie, who stood at the foot of the bed with her arms folded and a look of kindly determination on her face.

Amber was on her way out the door when another car pulled into the drive. She said, "Looks like you have more company. Don't overdo it."

"I'm sure they aren't here to see me."

Looking out the door, Nettie said, "I believe that is Mrs. Zimmerman talking to Elam."

Katie sat up as hope surged in her heart. Had Mrs. Zimmerman been able to contact Matt? Was he on his way here? "Is she coming in?"

"No. It looks like she's leaving, but Elam is coming to the house."

Unwilling to let hope die, Katie threaded her fingers together and held on tight. As soon as Elam walked in and she saw his face, her last tiny reservoir of hope faded into nothingness. "He's not going to come, is he?"

Elam shook his head. "Mrs. Zimmerman's grandson says the family has gone abroad. He sent a computer message to Matt, but he hasn't answered."

Katie nodded. "I think I'd like to rest now."

She slipped down under the covers and turned her back on the people standing beside her bed.

From her place inside her small alcove in the corner of the kitchen, Katie could hear Nettie and her son speaking in hushed tones, and the sounds of housework taking place, but she was simply too tired to care what they were saying.

Her beautiful daughter was her whole world now. Rachel was all that mattered.

■ ■ ■ ■

It was the smell of cinnamon bread baking that woke Katie on the morning of the third day. She opened her eyes to the sight of bright morning light pouring in through the kitchen windows. Someone, Nettie perhaps, had moved the screen aside. Warm and comfortable beneath the quilts, Katie rested, feeling secure and safe for the first time in weeks. She knew it was an illusion, but one she desperately wanted to hold on to.

Nettie was busy pulling a pan of steaming hot bread from the oven with the corner of her apron. The mouthwatering smell was enough to make Katie's empty stomach sit up and take notice with a loud rumble. Nettie glanced her way and began to chuckle. "I reckon that means you feel *goot* enough to have a bite to eat."

"If it tastes as good as it smells, I may wolf down the whole loaf."

"You'll have to fight Elam for it. This is his favorite."

Katie sat up and swung her bare feet to the cool plank floor. As she did, the room dipped and swirled, causing her to shut her eyes and clutch the side of the mattress.

"Are you all right?"

Katie opened her eyes to find Nettie watching her with deep concern. "Just a touch of dizziness. It's gone now."

"You sit right there until I get a cup of hot coffee into you. I don't want you fainting when you stand up."

Katie took several deep breaths and waited for the room to stop spinning. When everything settled into place, she looked down at her daughter sleeping quietly in her basket. The sight brought a thrill of delight to Katie's heart. This was her child, her gift. Matt had been wrong when he said a baby would only be a burden.

If he saw Rachel now, would it change how he felt? The thought pushed a lump of regret into her throat. She had made so many bad decisions.

Nettie, having poured the coffee from a dark blue, enameled pot on the back of the stove, laced it liberally with milk from a small pitcher on the table and added a spoonful of sugar before carrying the white earthenware mug to Katie.

Katie didn't take her coffee sweetened, but she didn't mention the fact. Nettie had done far too much for her. Grasping the cup, Katie sipped the hot drink slowly, feeling the warmth seep into her bones.

Nettie stood over her with her hands fisted

on her hips. Looking up, Katie said, "I'm fine. Really."

"I will tell you when you are fine. When the color comes back to those cheeks you can get up. Not before. Now drink."

"Yes, ma'am." Katie blew on the cup to cool the beverage and took another sip.

Nettie nodded, then left the room. She returned a few minutes later with a large black shawl, which she wrapped around Katie's shoulders. That done, Nettie turned back to the stove.

Upending the bread pan, she dumped the loaf onto a cutting board and pulled a knife from a drawer. Cutting off thick slices, she transferred them to a plate. Setting the dish aside, she began breaking eggs in a bowl. "Are you drinking?" she asked without looking.

"Yes." Katie took another quick sip and pulled the shawl tighter, grateful for its soft warmth.

She thought she detected a smile tugging at the corner of the older woman's mouth, but she didn't have a clear view of Nettie's face.

After a few minutes of silence, Nettie asked, "How's the coffee?"

"It's good. Better than my sister-in-law ever made on that stove. I used to think her bitter coffee gave Beatrice her sour face."

"You don't like your sister-in-law?"

"She's okay." It was more that Beatrice didn't like her. Katie had felt Beatrice's resentment from the moment she came to live with them, although she never understood why.

"I've got a sister-in-law I don't care for. It's not right to speak ill of her, but she thought my brother married up when he married into her family. That, and she claims her peach preserves are better than mine. They aren't. I use my mama's recipe."

"And riper peaches?"

Nettie's eyes brimmed with humor as she shot a look in Katie's direction. "Can you keep a secret?"

Taken aback slightly, Katie replied, "I guess. Sure."

"I use canned, store-bought peaches."

Katie laughed, feeling oddly pleased to be let in on a Sutter family joke.

Chuckling, Nettie continued. "I hate to think of the hours that woman has slaved over a hot stove stewing her fresh fruit and trying to outdo me. It's prideful, I know. I reckon I'd better confess my sin before next communion."

Katie's mirth evaporated. She bowed her head. She had so much more than a little false pride to confess. What must Nettie think of her?

If Mrs. Sutter hoped her admission would prompt Katie to seek acceptance back among the Amish, she was sadly mistaken. Katie had no intention of talking to a bishop or anyone else about the choices she'd made in her life. She had made them. She would live with them.

After a few minutes of silence, Nettie said, "It must feel strange to see another family living in your childhood home."

Relieved by the change of subject, Katie looked up to find her hostess watching her closely. "It was a bit of a shock."

"It's a good house, but I'd like a bigger porch. Elam has promised to build it this summer. I love to sit outside in the evenings and do my mending. That way I can enjoy a cup of coffee and the flowers in my garden while I watch the sun go down. Speaking of coffee, are you finished with yours?"

"Almost. Do you miss the home you left behind?"

"*Jah,* at times I do, but my oldest son and his wife still live on our farm in Pennsylvania, so I can go back for a visit as often as I like."

"What made you leave?"

A fleeting look of sadness crossed Nettie

face. "Elam wanted to come west. There's more farm ground out here and it's cheaper than back home. That, and there was some church trouble."

Nettie busied herself at the stove and began scrambling eggs in a large cast-iron skillet. Katie waited for her to elaborate, but she didn't. Although Katie found herself curious to hear more of the story, it was clear Nettie wasn't willing to share.

Suddenly, Nettie began speaking again. "My daughter-in-law's parents were talking about moving into the *dawdy haus* with one of their children. I would have welcomed the company, but then Elam told me he'd found this property."

The Amish welcomed their elderly relatives and nearly all Amish farms had a second, smaller, "grandfather house" connected to the main home. Grandparents could live in comfort and remain a part of the family, helping to care for the children or with the farm work if they were able.

"Elam is my youngest, you know, and he's without a wife yet. All my others are married. It just made sense for me to come with him and to keep house for him until he finds a wife of his own."

"Not all men want to get married." Katie was thinking more of Matt than Elam, but she did wonder why Nettie's son was still single. Besides being a handsome man, he was kind, gentle and seemed to love children.

Nettie stopped stirring and stared out the window. "Elam was betrothed once."

Katie recalled Elam's comment about "once burned, twice shy" the first night when he was holding Rachel. Now she knew what he meant. "What happened?"

Nettie began stirring her eggs again. "Salome wasn't the right one for him. It was better that they found it out before they were married, because she left the church."

"After her baptism?"

"Jah."

Katie knew what that meant. "She was shunned."

"It was very hard on Elam. Especially after . . ." Nettie paused and stared out the kitchen window as though seeing unhappy things in the past.

"You don't need to explain anything to me," Katie said, gently. She considered Nettie a friend, and she was willing to respect her privacy.

Nettie glanced her way. The sorrow-filled look in her eyes touched Katie's heart deeply. "It is no secret. You may hear it anyway. I'd rather you heard it from me.

66

My husband also left the church a few months before he died."

While the Amish religion might not be something Katie wanted for herself, she understood how deeply spiritual true believers were and how painful such an event would be to Nettie's entire family. "I'm so sorry."

"*Danki.* How are you feeling?"

"Better."

It was true. Katie finished her drink, rose and carried her cup to the table, happy to find her dizziness didn't return. As she sat down she thought she understood better why Elam disliked that she had left the faith. "That can't have been easy for Elam or for any of you."

Nettie looked over her shoulder with a sad little smile. "Life is not meant to be easy, child. That is why we pray for God's strength to help us bear it."

Katie didn't want to depend on God for her strength. She had made her own mistakes. She was the one who would fix them.

The front door opened and Elam came in accompanied by a draft of chilly air. In his arms he held a small bassinet. He paused when he caught sight of Katie at the table. She could have sworn that a blush crept up his neck, but she decided she was mistaken.

He nodded in her direction, then closed the door.

Nettie transferred her eggs from the stove top to a shallow bowl. "I was just getting ready to call you, Elam. Breakfast is ready."

"*Goot,* I could use some coffee. The wind has a raw bite to it this morning. March is not going out like a lamb. At least the sun is shining. The ground will be glad of the moisture when this snow melts. It will help our spring planting."

He hung his coat and black felt hat on the row of pegs beside the door, then he approached Katie. "I made your Rachel a better bed. It'll be safer than setting her basket on a chair and it will keep her up off the drafty floor."

The bassinet was about a third the size of the ones Katie had seen in the stores in the city when she had gone window-shopping and dreamed about things she could never afford for her baby. The picnic basket–size bed was finely crafted of wooden strips sanded smooth and glowing with a linseed oil finish. It had a small canopy at one end. "It's lovely. You didn't have to do this."

"It was easy enough to make out of a few things I had on hand. It has double swing handles and the legs fold up so you can take it with you when you leave. Have you had

68

time to write a letter to your brother? I'll carry it to the mailbox for you."

He wasn't exactly pushing her out the door, but he was making it plain she couldn't expect to stay longer than necessary.

She didn't blame him. Katie knew she had been dependent on the Sutters' charity for too long already. She'd never intended to take advantage of them and yet she was.

How could she explain that her brother — her only family — wouldn't come to her aid? She might find shelter for herself and her baby at his home, but it would be on his terms and his terms alone.

Elam was waiting for her answer. She wouldn't lie to him. Nor could she write and pretend she was waiting for an answer when she knew full well the letter would come back unopened.

She glanced at Elam. Two important people in his life had betrayed the faith and he had shunned them.

If he knew her brother had disowned her would he allow her to stay?

CHAPTER FIVE

"Let the girl get a little food in her before you start pestering her, Elam."

Elam didn't miss the grateful look Katie flashed at his mother. He kept silent, but only out of respect for Nettie. His unexpected visitor had aroused his curiosity and a niggling sense of unease. Katie didn't seem at all eager to contact her brother. That bothered him.

That and Grace Zimmerman's comments about Malachi's harsh treatment of his young sister.

Elam was well aware that some men held to the idea that being the head of the house gave them the right to be stern, even cruel. He also knew such behavior was against God's teaching.

If Katie had been subjected to that type of treatment in the past, it might explain a lot. But even if her life had been difficult, it was no excuse for turning her back on her religion.

Nor was it his place to pass judgment on her or on her brother, he reminded himself sternly. He stepped up to the sink and began to wash. When he was finished, he pulled a white towel off the hook on the end of the counter and dried his hands.

Whatever troubles Katie had, she would take them with her when she left. Then the peace he tried so hard to cultivate would once again return to his life.

Nettie set a bowl in the center of the table. "Take a seat, both of you. Don't let my eggs get cold."

Elam took his place at the head of the table, and Nettie sat in her usual spot at his right. Katie was already seated in the chair to his left. In the morning light her color was still pale, made more so by the black woolen shawl she had wrapped about her shoulders. The dark circles under her eyes added to the impression of sadness he saw in her face.

Her dark eyes looked too big for her thin face. What she needed was some of his mother's good cooking to put a little meat on her bones. He wasn't a man who liked scrawny women.

She quietly clasped her hands together and bowed her head. The movement sent

71

the ends of her short hair swinging against her cheeks. The sight brought a sudden tightening to his chest. She might be a thin waif, but she was also a woman. There was no mistaking that or the odd pull of attraction he felt when she was near.

He tore his gaze away. He'd made a fool of himself over a woman once before and once was enough. Closing his eyes, he bowed his head as a signal to the others, then he began a silent blessing over the meal.

When he was finished, he cleared his throat to signal the prayer was done, then reached for the cinnamon bread. Katie stretched out her arm at the same moment and their hands touched. He felt the shock of the contact all the way up his arm.

She jerked her hand back as quickly as he did. A flush stained her cheeks, giving her back some much-needed color.

"I'm sorry," he mumbled. "Help yourself."

"You first. You've been out working already."

"And you're eating for two."

Following their exchange neither of them moved. Finally Nettie pushed the plate closer to Katie. "I thought you were starving?"

Katie smiled shyly at her. "I am."

"Then eat," Elam added sternly. When Katie still didn't move he took her plate and loaded it with scrambled eggs, two sausage patties and two thick slices of cinnamon bread. When the plate was filled to his satisfaction, he set it in front of her and folded his arms over his chest.

Her blush deepened, but she picked up her fork and began eating. She kept her head down and her gaze focused on her meal so she didn't see the look of triumph on his mother's face, but Elam did.

He had seen just that look when his mother had convinced his oldest sister that her two boys needed and deserved to keep the muddy stray puppy they'd found in the orchard on their last visit. His mother had a big heart and she often thought she knew what was best for everyone.

In the case of the puppy she had been right, but her desire to mother Katie and her little girl wasn't the same thing at all. Having Katie in their home could easily bring the censure of the community to bear on them. Katie's rejection of her faith placed all of them in an awkward position. He and his mother had few friends among their new acquaintances who would speak up for them.

His mother had endured enough heartache back in Pennsylvania. He wanted it to be different here.

From the far corner of the room, Rachel began crying. Katie quickly started to rise, but Nettie stopped her by saying, "I'll get her this time. You finish your meal."

Katie sank back into her seat. "Thank you."

Elam noticed she didn't take her eyes off Rachel as his mother picked the child up. Nettie said, "I see what's wrong, *moppel.* You need your diaper changed."

She carried the child to her bedroom as she crooned, "We had better send Elam to the store for more."

Elam turned his attention back to Katie. "If you make a list of things you need I'll be happy to make a trip into town."

She stared at her plate and pushed a piece of sausage around with her fork. "I don't have the money to repay you."

"I asked for a list, not for money. Your brother will settle with me when he comes for you. I'm not worried about it."

When she made no comment, he resumed eating, but she didn't. The silence in the room lengthened uncomfortably. Every time he brought up the subject of her brother she clammed up. He wasn't sure what to make of her withdrawal. He wasn't sure

74

what to make of Katie Lantz at all.

He could understand her reluctance to admit to her family how far she had fallen, but the time for such false pride was past. She had a child to care for now and no way that he could see to support herself, let alone her baby. If she couldn't bring herself to write her brother then Elam would do it for her.

That might be best. He could mail a letter today.

He would not include the details of her plight. That would be for Katie to do. He'd only say that she had come looking for her family and that she needed her brother's assistance to get home.

When Katie found the courage she could say what she needed to say to her family, but the sooner they came for her the better it would be for everyone.

Elam studied her as she picked at her food. He'd heard not one word of complaint from her. She didn't bemoan her fate, that was commendable. She was certainly attentive to her baby. The love she had for her child shone in her eyes whenever she looked upon her babe's face. There was much he liked about Katie. It was a pity she had turned her back on the Plain life.

As if aware of his scrutiny, she self-consciously tucked her hair behind her ear, then gave up any pretense of eating. She laid her fork down and folded her hands in her lap. "I'll make a list of things the baby needs. It won't be much."

"*Goot.* Now eat or my mother will scold us both." He gestured toward her plate with his fork.

A hint of a smile tugged at her lips, but it vanished quickly. She picked up her slice of cinnamon bread and took a dainty bite.

A few minutes later, Nettie returned with a quiet baby nestled in her arms. Katie started to rise. "I'll take her."

Nettie waved her away. "I can manage. You've barely touched your food."

"And you haven't eaten a thing," Katie countered.

Elam pushed his empty plate aside. "I'll take her, then you can both eat."

"Very well." Nettie handed Rachel over reluctantly.

Elam took her and settled her upright against his shoulder. He liked holding her. Leaning back in his chair, he glanced down at her plump cheeks and tiny mouth. Each day it was easier to see the resemblance between her and her mother, except Katie's cheeks were hollow, not plump and healthy-looking. They shared the same full bottom lip, but Rachel's curved naturally into a sweet smile.

His gaze was drawn to Katie's face. She was watching him, an odd expression in her eyes. What would it take to make her smile as freely as her baby did?

Katie returned to her bed for the rest of the day. Physically she was stronger, but when night finally came the hopelessness of her situation pulled her spirits to a new low. She was homeless and penniless with a new baby to care for and a growing debt to the people that had befriended her.

The memory of Nettie and Elam's tender care of Rachel brought tears to her eyes. For one horrible instant she wondered if her baby wouldn't be better off without her.

Turning over, she muffled her sobs in the pillow as she gave in to despair.

The following morning she stayed behind the screen until Elam had gone outside. She didn't want to answer his questions about why she hadn't written to Malachi. It was cowardly and she knew she couldn't avoid the subject much longer, but she didn't know how to explain.

She had been a trial to Malachi and his wife all her life. Even though the Sutters were aware she had made bad choices, she didn't want them to know Malachi had disowned her. She was too ashamed to admit it. If she had to grovel before Malachi, for her child's sake she would, but what little pride she had left kept her from admitting as much to the Sutter family.

The day passed slowly, but when Elam came in for supper he didn't mention her brother or ask her for a letter. Relieved, but puzzled, she was able to eat a little of Nettie's excellent beef stew and listen as Elam talked about plans for planting pumpkins to sell in addition to their normal produce.

"Pumpkins?" Nettie cocked her head to the side. "Would you sell them through the organic farming co-op?"

"*Jah.* The demand is growing."

Katie's curiosity was aroused. She knew most of the area's Amish farmers sold their produce from roadside stands and at the local produce auctions. Every year her brother had complained bitterly about how hard it was to earn a living competing against the large, mechanized English farms. She asked, "What's an organic co-op?"

Nettie passed a bowl of her canned pears to Katie. "Last year Elam persuaded several dozen farmers to switch from conventional agriculture to organic, using no chemicals, no antibiotics, none of those things."

Katie could see the spark of interest in his eyes. "There's a good market for organic vegetables, fruits and cheeses. I had heard about such a co-op near Akron. Aaron Zook and I contacted them. They helped us find a chain of grocery stores in Cleveland that were interested in selling our crops. They even helped us obtain our organic certification from the U.S.D.A."

"The government men came and inspected the barns and the fields of everyone involved," Nettie added.

Frowning slightly, Katie asked, "Isn't it more expensive to farm that way?"

He gave a slight shake of his head. "Not if it's done right."

"Elam attended seminars on soil management to learn what organic products would give our soil the best nutrients. He learned how to make the plants strong, so they wouldn't fall prey to insects and disease without chemicals to protect them. It has already saved two of our families from losing their farms." Nettie beamed, clearly pleased with her son's accomplishments.

It seemed there was more to Elam than the stoic farmer Katie had assumed he was. The Amish were known as shrewd businessmen, but it was plain Elam was also forward thinking.

Nettie picked up her empty plate and carried it to the sink. "If our people can make a living from the farms and not have to work in factories, then our families will stay intact. It's a win-win situation."

After the meal was over Nettie retired to her sewing room, and in what seemed like no time she emerged with a stack of baby gowns for Rachel and two new cotton nightgowns for Katie.

"You shouldn't have." Katie managed to speak past the lump of gratitude in her throat.

Nettie smiled. "You might as well accept them. They're much too small for me and I'm not going to rip out all those stitches."

It seemed that every minute Katie stayed here she became more indebted to Elam and his mother. She needed to be on her way. It was doubtful that Malachi would pay back any of the money the Sutters had spent on her or Rachel. In time, when she found a job, she would make sure she repaid them herself as soon as possible.

The following days passed in much the same fashion. Katie took care of Rachel and tried to regain her strength. Nettie fussed over the both of them.

Whatever Elam thought of Nettie's pampering, he kept it to himself, but Katie could tell he was ready for her to be on her way. Elam had done his Christian duty by taking her in, but he wanted her out of his home. He avoided looking at her when he was in the same room. A faint scowl creased his brows whenever his gaze did fall on her.

Nearly a week after her arrival, Katie was helping clear the lunch dishes when Nettie announced that she and Elam were driving her out to her daughter Mary's farm some five miles away. That explained why Nettie had been baking all morning.

"Mary is pregnant and expecting in a few months. She's been feeling low. I've several baskets of baked goods and preserves I want to take her and her family. Nothing makes a person feel more chipper than a good shoofly pie they didn't have to bake themselves."

Grateful as Katie was for Nettie's care and mothering, she was excited to hear she would finally have some time alone. "When will you be back?"

"I think about four o'clock. Will you be okay without us? I could have Elam stay with you."

"No, I'll be fine."

"I'm sure you will. You should rest. You still look washed-out."

"Oh, thank you very much." Katie rolled her eyes, and Nettie chuckled.

Thirty minutes later, with Rachel asleep and the quietness of the house pressing in, Katie put down the book she couldn't get into and began looking for something to do. Memories of her life in this same house crept out without Nettie's happy chatter to keep them at bay.

It wasn't so much that her brother had been cruel. It was that he had been cold and devoid of the love she saw so freely given by Nettie to her son. The Sutters were the kind of family Katie longed to be a part of. Malachi and his wife hadn't given her that. Neither had Matt.

With sudden clarity, Katie realized she would have to see that Rachel grew up knowing she was loved, knowing happiness and hearing laughter. A new determination pushed aside the pity she had been wallowing in. She would raise her child on her own. She would get a job and make a life for the two of them. They would have to live with Malachi for a while, but it wouldn't be any longer than absolutely necessary.

Katie walked into the kitchen with a new sense of purpose. In her rush to leave, Nettie had left a few pots and pans soaking in the sink. Smiling, Katie pushed up the sleeves of her sweater and carried a kettle to the sink. She filled it with water and put it on the stove to heat. It was time to stop feeling sorry for herself and do something for someone else.

It wasn't long until she was putting the last clean pot in the cupboard and closing the door. Looking around the spotless kitchen, she bit the corner of her lower lip. Would Nettie think it was clean enough? Would Elam?

That was a silly thought. Why should she want to impress Elam with how well she could manage a home? He wouldn't care. He wasn't at all like Malachi.

Many was the time she'd scrubbed this same kitchen until her hands were raw only to have her brother come in, look around and begin shouting that she couldn't do anything right, that if she wanted to live in filth she could live in the barn.

How many nights had she spent locked inside the feed room listening to the sounds of scurrying mice in the darkness? Too many to count.

She pressed a hand to her lips to hide the tiny smile that crept out of hiding. Malachi would have been furious to know she hadn't really minded sleeping there. The old sheet she had been given was much softer stuffed with hay than the thin mattress in her room upstairs. The mice had been quieter than her brother's heavy snoring in the room next to hers. She often wondered how her sister-in-law ever got a wink of sleep.

Folding the dish towel carefully, Katie hung it on the towel bar at the end of the counter. Nettie and Elam were not like Malachi. She didn't have to be afraid while she was here.

Two hours later Katie's solitude was interrupted when Amber arrived to check on her patients. To Katie's chagrin, the nurse caught her sweeping the porch and steps free of the mud that clung to everything now that the weather had warmed up enough to melt the snow.

Amber advanced on Katie and took the broom out of her hands. "What do you think you're doing? I gave you strict orders to rest."

Katie sighed. "I'm not used to lying around. Besides, I wanted to repay Nettie's kindness in some small fashion. She and Elam have gone to visit his sister and I thought I'd clean up a little while she was gone."

"I understand, but you won't repay her if you overdo it and get sick. That will just make more work for her. Come inside and have a seat. I want to check your blood pressure. At least your color is better today."

"I feel fine." Maybe if she kept repeating the phrase it would remain true.

Inside the house, Katie hung up her coat and took a seat at the kitchen table. Amber did the same and opened the large canvas bag she carried slung over one shoulder. "How's your appetite?"

"It's good."

Amber narrowed her eyes as she wrapped the black cuff around Katie's arm. "If I ask Nettie, what will she say?"

"She'll say I pick at my food like a bird."

"I thought so." Placing her stethoscope in her ears, Amber inflated the cuff and took her reading.

"Well?" Katie asked when she was done.

"It's good, and your pulse is normal, too. You Amish women amaze me the way you bounce back after childbirth."

"I'm not Amish."

"I'm sorry. That was thoughtless of me." Amber leaned back to regard Katie intently. "I know you grew up here and I've lived in Hope Springs for almost six years, yet I don't remember seeing you."

"How can you tell us apart in our white caps and dark dresses?" Katie didn't mean to sound bitter, but she couldn't help it.

"I think I would have remembered you. There aren't too many women in this area with black hair and eyes as dark as yours. I don't think I remember your brother and his wife."

"They didn't have any children."

"Then they'll be excited to have a baby in the house."

"I'm not so sure."

Amber leaned forward and placed a hand on Katie's arm. "I will tell you something I've learned in my years as a nurse midwife. No matter how upset a family may be at the circumstances surrounding the arrival of a baby, once that child is born . . . the love just comes pouring out. It's the way God made us."

Would that be the case for her and Rachel? Would her daughter bring love and happiness to her brother's home? Would Rachel help her mother find the sense of belonging she craved?

They were big hopes to pin on such a small baby.

One step at a time, Katie cautioned herself. First, she had to get home, and soon. She had been a burden on the Sutters long enough.

"Amber, do you know what day the bus

leaves that I'd need to take to go to Kansas?"

"As a matter of fact I keep copies of the bus schedule in my car. You have no idea how often I'm asked about that when people want to make plans for family members to come see a new baby. I should just memorize it. It isn't like Hope Springs is a major hub. I think we only get four buses a week through here."

After she checked on Rachel, Amber went out to her car and returned with a laminated sheet of paper. "It looks like the bus going west leaves on Monday and Friday evening at six-ten. The buses going east leave on Wednesday and Saturday afternoon at five forty-five. There's no Sunday service."

Today was Friday. Katie glanced at the clock. It was half past two now. If she hurried, she could make today's bus. Otherwise, she wouldn't be able to leave until Monday. As much as she had grown to like Nettie and even Elam, she didn't want to burden them with her presence for three more days.

The only problem was that she was broke. She didn't have enough money to pay for a ticket to the next town, let alone to go across four states.

Amber tucked the sheet in her bag. "Actually, the bus isn't the best way for you to travel. The best thing would be if your brother could arrange to send a car."

The Amish often hired drivers for long trips. It was a common occurrence in a society devoted to the horse and buggy. One was permitted to ride in an automobile for such things as doctor visits or to travel to see relatives that lived far away. One could even take an airplane if they obtained the bishop's permission.

Katie had heard that a few Amish churches permitted owning and driving a car, but that certainly wasn't accepted by her brother's church. "Hiring a driver to come all this way would be expensive."

Amber fisted her hands on her hips. "True, but you can tell your brother that's what the nurse recommends."

Katie forced a smile, but she knew her brother wouldn't send anyone for her. She would have to make her own way home.

Only . . . what if she didn't go. What if she stayed in Hope Springs?

The kindness and caring she'd been shown over the last few days had given her a different vision of what her life could be like. A new sense of energy swept through her. "Amber, do you know of any jobs in the area?"

"For you?"

"Yes. Perhaps someone who needs live-in help. I'm not afraid of hard work. I can clean and cook. I know my way around a farm. I'll take anything."

"I don't know of any work right offhand, but I'll keep my ears open. Are you thinking of returning to Hope Springs?"

"I just need a job as soon as possible."

Stepping close, Amber laid a hand on Katie's arm. Her eyes softened. "If you're worried about paying me, don't be. I can wait."

She pulled a card from her coat pocket. "This is my address. Just send what you can . . . when you can."

Katie took the card, but her heart sank. It seemed that God wanted her to return to her brother's house after all. She considered asking Amber for the loan of enough money to reach her brother's but quickly discarded the idea. She already owed the woman for her midwife services. She couldn't ask for anything else. Except perhaps a ride into town.

"Amber, are you heading back to Hope Springs now?"

Taking her coat from the hook by the door, Amber slipped it on and lifted her long blond hair from beneath it, letting it spill down her back. "No, I've got a few more visits to make. I'm on my way to check on Mrs. Yoder and her new baby. I'm worried that the child is jaundiced. I may end up sending them to the hospital. Why? Was there something you needed in town?"

Katie shook her head. "It's nothing that can't wait until the Sutters get home."

"Are you sure?"

"I'm sure."

After Amber left, Katie pulled out the newspaper that Nettie had finished reading that morning. Quickly, she looked over the help wanted ads in case there was something listed that Amber didn't know about. As she read the few listings her heart sank. There were few jobs available, and none for a woman without education or skills.

Folding the paper, Katie returned it to Nettie's reading table. Rachel began crying in the other room. Katie picked her up and sat on the edge of her bed. "I feel like crying, too."

So much for her renewed sense of optimism.

Looking around the room, Katie couldn't believe how much she had dreaded coming to this place. Now she dreaded leaving. In a strange way her arrival here had turned out to be a blessing. What else could she call this family's kindness?

Cradling her baby, she looked down at her child's wonderful bright eyes and beautiful face. "I just have to believe that God has more blessings in store for us when we reach Malachi's new home."

Reaching that home would require money they didn't have. Besides her clothes and shoes, she didn't own anything of value. As much as she dreaded it, she would simply have to tell Elam why she hadn't yet written to Malachi.

Perhaps Elam and Nettie knew of some work she could do to earn her bus fare. No doubt Nettie would offer to pay Katie's way home, but she couldn't take advantage of the woman's kind heart any more than she already had.

After feeding her daughter, Katie laid the baby in her bassinet. "At least you own a fine place to sleep. Never take it for granted."

Lifting the handles, Katie started to carry the baby's bed into the living room, but stopped in the doorway and looked down. She did own something of value. The bed Elam had made for Rachel was beautifully crafted, but was it worth more than a bus ticket out of town?

Could she bring herself to sell it?

No, Elam had made it clear that it was a

gift to Rachel. He'd even made it to travel, so Katie could take it with her.

She bit her lip. Selling it would solve her immediate problem. Should she?

The memory of Elam gently holding her baby in the moonlight came rushing to mind.

His kindness to her daughter had touched something deep inside Katie. Thoughts of him stirred vague longings, but she refused to examine those feelings. She had no right to be thinking about her own happiness. Rachel was her first priority.

Malachi would give them a home where Rachel would be safe. She'd have a roof over her head and food to eat. What did it matter that her mother had coldhearted relatives? Rachel would be taken care of and one day soon they would both leave again. For good.

Katie sat in the chair before the fireplace and considered her options. The weather was decently warm today. She would make sure Rachel was snugly dressed and wrapped in one of Nettie's old but warm quilts. As soon as she could, Katie would send the quilt back with a letter of thanks for its use.

It was only a three-mile walk into town. She could easily get there before the bus left that evening. Unless things had changed drastically in Hope Springs, there were several stores in town that catered to the tourist trade by selling Amish furniture, gifts and quilts. The thought of parting with Elam's beautiful gift gave Katie pause, but she didn't see any other choice.

No. This was the only way.

CHAPTER SIX

It was nearly four o'clock in the afternoon when Elam and his mother returned home. Leaving Judy tied up near the gate, he helped his mother unload her empty baskets and carried them up the steps for her. Inside the front door, he stopped. The house had an odd, empty feel to it.

He glanced around the kitchen. The folding screen had been pushed back against the wall. Katie's bed was stripped and empty. The quilts and sheets sat neatly folded at one end. Rachel's cradle was gone along with Katie's suitcase. It was clear they had left.

His heart sank. He'd tried not to become attached to them, but it seemed that he had failed.

Nettie came in behind him. "Just set those baskets on the table, son. I'll get them washed in a few minutes. Are you still planning to go to the lumberyard?"

He didn't move, couldn't take his eyes off the empty corner. "Yes. I need to pick up some more cedar to finish the chest I'm working on."

Where had she gone? Had she found someone to take her to her family or was she going back to the city and Rachel's father?

"What's wrong?" Nettie asked as she stepped around him.

"I think our little birds have flown." He couldn't believe how disappointed he was. In only a few days he'd become deeply attached to little Rachel . . . and to her mother, although he hated to admit that, even to himself.

Walking to the table, he set the baskets on it and slipped one hand into his pants pocket. He withdrew the pink-and-white wooden baby rattle he'd made and simply stared at it.

"She can't be gone." His mother's distress was clear as she carried her burdens in and set them next to his. A letter sat in the middle of the table. Nettie picked it up and read it.

She pulled her bonnet from her head and laid it and the note on the table, then turned to Elam. "That girl doesn't have a lick of sense. She isn't strong enough to be gadding about. She's gone to the bus station. You have to go after her."

That was exactly what he wanted to do. He wanted to bring her back where she and her baby would be safe, but perhaps this was for the best. Perhaps it was better that Katie went away before he grew any fonder of her and her child. He knew what heartbreak lay in that direction.

"She's a grown woman, *Mamm.* She has made up her mind."

"She's not thinking straight. She's putting herself and her baby in danger."

"What do you mean?"

"The baby blues have muddled her thinking. Tell me you didn't notice how depressed she has been. What if she collapses on the way, or worse?"

"The town is only three miles away. Amish children walk that far to school every day." He slipped the rattle back in his pocket.

"Please, take the buggy and fetch her back. It will get cold as soon as the sun goes down."

"By then she'll be on a bus headed for Kansas. She will be happier with her own family."

Nettie paced the length of the kitchen and back with her hands pressed to her cheeks. "I'm not sure that's true."

He frowned. "Do you know something you aren't telling me?"

"It's not what I know. It's what I feel. She didn't want to write to her brother. Why? Something isn't right."

"You can't know that."

"Even if I'm wrong, we at least need to make sure she made it to the bus depot. I couldn't rest without knowing that she and that precious baby are all right. Katie isn't strong enough to be traveling. What will become of Rachel if anything happens to her mother?"

Everything Nettie said was an echo of his own concerns, but still he hesitated. "Katie has the right to live her own life as she sees fit. She has made her choice. She chose to leave us."

He turned to the bed in the corner and began dragging off the mattress.

"Elam, what are you doing?"

"I'm putting the bed back in the spare bedroom. We have no need of it in here anymore."

The little bassinet, which seemed like such a wonderful way to carry Rachel, had become horribly heavy long before Katie had finished the first mile. By the time she reached the outskirts of town she'd already stopped to rest a dozen times. Now, outside the Amish Trading Post, she simply had to stop again.

After setting Rachel down gently on the sidewalk, Katie used her suitcase as a seat. Rubbing her aching arms, she willed her nagging dizziness away. She was stronger than this. She had to be.

The hollowness in the pit of her stomach made her wish she'd had the forethought to bring something to eat. The sun was low in the western sky and the chill had returned to the air. She had no idea what time it was, but it was getting late. She couldn't rest for long. She had to make it to the bus station on time.

Glancing down, the sight of her sleeping daughter brought a little smile to Katie's lips. At least the baby had slept the whole trip. Lifting Rachel from the bassinet, Katie swaddled her tightly in her blanket. Rising, she pushed her suitcase beneath the branches of a nearby cedar tree, picked up Elam's gift and crossed the street to the store.

At the door, she hesitated. Rachel's bed was the only thing she owned that had been given to her out of kindness. Keeping it meant hanging on to a small part of Elam.

No, I've already been over this. It has to be

done. Open the door and go in.

Selling the bassinet proved to be easier than she had hoped. In fact, the woman behind the counter asked if Katie could supply her with several more. Pocketing the cash, Katie thanked the saleswoman and gave her Elam's name. If she helped him earn some extra income, it might make up in some small way for the fact that she'd had to part with his gift like this.

Once outside the building, Katie retrieved her suitcase and hurried toward the bus station. Main Street in Hope Springs ran north and south past shops, a café and small, neat homes with drab winter yards. Traffic was light. Only an occasional car passed her. Each time she heard the fast clip-clop of a buggy coming up behind her she couldn't help but think of Elam and Nettie and how kind they had been to her.

In a secret place in her heart, Katie foolishly wished that Elam would come after her. She knew better, but the wish remained.

She prayed he and his mother were not offended by her abrupt departure. She'd tried to explain herself in the note she'd left, but words were inadequate to thank them for all they had done.

The bus depot lay at the far side of town just off the highway. Relief flooded through her when she saw the large blue and gray vehicle still idling beneath the corrugated iron awning outside the terminal. A man in a gray uniform was stowing a green duffel bag in the luggage compartment. She stopped beside him. "Is this the bus going west?"

"It is."

"Can I still get a ticket?"

He slammed the storage lid shut. "If you hurry. I'm pulling out in five minutes."

"I'll hurry."

Inside, she rushed to the ticket window, but had to wait for a couple, obviously tourists, to finish first. She glanced repeatedly at the large clock on the wall.

When it was finally her turn, she said, "I need a ticket to Yoder, Kansas."

The short, bald man with glasses didn't look up, but typed away at his keyboard. "We don't have service to Yoder. The nearest town is Hutchinson, Kansas. You'll have to make connections in St. Louis and Kansas City."

"That will be fine. How much is it?" She pulled the bills from her pocket.

"One hundred and sixty-nine dollars."

Her heart dropped to her feet. That was thirty dollars more than she had. This couldn't be happening. She'd come so far.

She'd even sold Elam's gift to her child. Rachel began squirming and fussing. Tightening her grip on her daughter, Katie said, "Are you sure it's that much?"

He looked over his glasses. "I'm sure. Do you want a ticket or not?"

"I don't have enough, but I have to get on this bus." What was she going to do?

"We take credit cards."

"I don't have one," she admitted in a small voice.

"Then I can't sell you a ticket. I'm sorry."

"Please, I have to get on this bus today."

"Do you want to buy a ticket to St. Louis instead of Hutchinson?" he suggested.

"No." What good would it do to arrive in a strange city with no money and no one to help her? It would be jumping from the frying pan into the fire. She turned to look over the waiting room. Besides the tourist, there were two Amish men, both in black suits with wide-brimmed, black felt hats and long gray beards. The only other person waiting to board was a young soldier in brown-and-green fatigues.

Rachel began crying in earnest. Any pride that Katie had slid away in the face of her growing desperation. She left the ticket counter and approached the Amish men first praying they would treat her with the same kindness the Sutter family had shown her.

"Sirs, I must get on this bus, but I don't have enough money to reach my destination. Could I beg you for the loan of thirty dollars? I will pay you back, I promise."

The men stared at her a long moment, then one spoke to the other in German, but Katie understood them. "She looks like a runaway. We shouldn't help her. We should send her back to her family."

"Jah."

The bus driver pushed open the outside door and said, "All aboard."

Katie clutched the black gabardine sleeve of the Amish elder. "I'm not a runaway. I mean . . . I was, but I'm trying to reach my brother's home. Malachi Lantz. Perhaps you knew him before he moved away from here."

"We are not from Hope Springs. We came on business and now we must go home." They picked up their satchels and moved toward the doorway.

Katie spun around to face the English tourists. "Please. I only need thirty more dollars to get home. Won't you help me?"

The man hesitated, then started to pull his wallet out of his pocket, but his wife stopped him. "She probably wants it for drug money. I've heard plenty stories about these Amish teenagers. Let's go."

Tears filled Katie's eyes as she watched them leave. The young soldier stopped at her side. "I've only got ten bucks on me, but you're welcome to it. I won't need it. I'm headed back to my post."

She shook her head. "It's not enough, but bless you."

He shrugged and said, "Good luck."

As the people filed up the steps of the bus outside, Katie sank onto one of the chairs. Exhaustion rushed in to sap what little strength she had left.

The man behind the ticket counter came out and began turning off the lights. "We're closing, ma'am. You'll have to leave."

Rising, she picked up her small suitcase and walked out with lagging steps.

The bus pulled away in a cloud of diesel fumes. The sight reminded her so much of her arrival only days ago that she started to laugh. Only her chuckle turned into a broken sob. She couldn't do anything right. Everything she touched turned to ashes. She couldn't run away. She couldn't even run home. How was she going to take care of her daughter?

Dropping her suitcase, she sat on it and leaned back against the wall of the depot. She pressed a hand to her lips to stifle the next sob.

Rachel began crying but Katie was too tired to do more than hold her. Closing her eyes, she rocked back and forth. "What will become of us now?"

CHAPTER SEVEN

Elam finished loading the lumber he needed into the back of his farm cart. His gray Belgian draft horse, Joey, stood quietly, his head hung low, waiting to carry the load home. As Elam closed the tailgate of the wagon, he heard someone call his name. Turning, he saw Bishop Joseph Zook approaching.

"Good evening to you, Elam." The bishop touched the brim of his black felt hat.

"And to you, Bishop," Elam replied, feeling uneasy at the man's intense scrutiny.

"Mrs. Zimmerman mentioned that Katie Lantz has been staying with you. I didn't know she was a friend of the family."

"She returned expecting to find her brother still farming here. The shock of finding him gone brought on her labor and she delivered a little girl, but they left today."

"She's gone, then?" The bishop seemed relieved.

"*Jah,* she's gone." Saying the words made it seem so final. Katie had dropped into his life without warning. She had stirred up feelings he'd tried to keep buried. Now she was gone and he felt her loss keenly.

He hesitated, then asked, "Did you know her well, Bishop?"

"I did not. Once she was of age, she rarely attended services or gatherings. Her brother used to lament how stubborn and how selfish she was, how she thought herself better than the others in our Plain community. He expressed much worry that she meant to leave us and to entice other youth away, as well."

Her brother's description didn't match the quiet, meek woman that had come to Elam's door. Still, her family would know her best.

Bishop Zook hooked his thumbs in his suspenders. "I wish that I might have spoken to her to see if she has come back to the faith. My cousin lives near Malachi in Kansas and he has written that they are happy in their new home. It would be good news for them to hear Katie has found redemption."

Elam shook his head. "She was in trouble and seeking her family's help, but I fear she does not mean to stay among the Plain people."

"It was commendable that you rendered her assistance, but it is better that she has left your home if she has not repented. Perhaps she will see the error of her ways. Until then all we can do is pray for her."

"*Jah,* we can do that. I'd best be getting on my way or it will be dark before I get home." Elam nodded toward the bishop and climbed up to his seat.

"Please tell your mother I send my regards."

"I will. She's looking forward to holding church services at our home come Sunday."

"I know God will bless the gathering. It will not be long until spring communion is upon us. We must select a new deacon before then."

"I was sorry to hear of Deacon Yoder's passing. I did not know him well, but I'm told he was a good man."

"He is with God now, and we must all rejoice in that."

Besides the bishop, Elam's church district had two preaching ministers and one deacon. The deacon's responsibilities included helping the bishop and preachers at church services and assisting needy members of the community, such as widows, by collecting alms. It was also the duty of a deacon to secure information about errant members of the community and convey those to the bishop.

It had been the deacon in Elam's old church that had brought the pronouncement of Elam's father's excommunication and later the news of his fiancée's shunning.

"You are new to our congregation, Elam. If you feel you don't know our men well enough to nominate someone for the office, I can offer you some guidance. My cousin in Kansas writes that they too have lost their deacon and that Malachi Lantz has been chosen to take his place."

Being single, Elam knew he was ineligible to be nominated, and for that he was glad. Only married men could serve. A deacon would be chosen by lots from among the nominated men. It was a lifelong appointment.

Nodding to the bishop, Elam said, "I will visit with you after services this Sunday."

Slapping the lines against Joey's broad rump, Elam left the lumberyard and headed down Lake Street toward Main. Pulling to a halt at the traffic light, he glanced up Main toward the bus depot at the other end of town. Had Katie already left? Was she on her way to her brother's or was she going back to the city and Rachel's father?

Either way it was none of his business, so

why did he care so much? The light turned green, but he didn't notice until a car honked behind him. The English, always in such a hurry.

He clucked his tongue to get Joey moving, but as they entered the intersection Elam suddenly turned the horse left instead of right.

What would it hurt to make sure Katie had gotten on the bus? If he could tell his mother he knew for certain Katie had left town Nettie might feel better and give up worrying over Katie and Rachel. He didn't closely examine his own motives for going out of his way. He simply assumed he wanted the chance to say goodbye.

As he neared the station, he saw the lights were off and the closed sign had been hung on the door. Sadness filled him. The bus had already gone, taking puzzling, pretty Katie Lantz with it.

Pulling on the reins, he started to turn around when he caught the sound of a baby crying. Drawing closer to the building, he saw Katie sitting huddled against the side of the depot. She had her head down, her face buried in one hand as she cradled her baby with the other. Her shoulders shook with heavy sobs.

He stopped the wagon and jumped down.

Reaching her in three long strides, he dropped to his haunches beside her.

Her head jerked up and he found himself looking at her red-rimmed eyes and tearstained face, partially obscured by the curtain of her dark hair. Even in her pitiful state he couldn't help but think how beautiful she was. Reaching out with one hand, he gently tucked her hair behind her ear. "Ah, Katie, why couldn't you have been on that bus."

"I tried . . . but I didn't have . . . enough money."

Her broken sobs twisted his heart like a wet dishrag. He had no business caring so much about this woman. He said, "Mother wants me to bring you home."

"I can't . . . go with you. I've been . . . too much trouble . . . already. We'll be . . . fine."

"You are a prideful woman, Katie. Would you stop me from doing what the Bible commands of me?"

At her look of confusion, he said, "It is my duty to care for anyone who is destitute and in need, even if it be my bitter enemy — which you are not. Now, let me have Rachel." He eased the baby from her arms.

"Besides, if Mother found out that I left you and Rachel here alone she would tan my hide. Or make me do my own cooking, which would be worse." His attempt at humor brought a fresh onslaught of crying.

"Don't cry, Katie." Slipping his free hand under her elbow, he helped her to her feet. She swayed, and for a second he feared she would crumple to the sidewalk. He pulled her close to steady her, wondering how he could manage to carry both of them to the wagon.

"Be strong just a little longer," he whispered.

She nodded and moved away from him, but he didn't let go of her arm. Helping her up onto the wagon seat, he glanced toward the street as a horse and buggy trotted past. What kind of rumors would soon be flying about him and the weeping English woman he'd picked up at the bus station? Hope Springs was a small town with a well-oiled rumor mill. By tomorrow, speculation would be flying over the fences.

More gossip was the last thing he wanted for his family in their new community, but leaving Katie and her baby on the side of the road was out of the question. He briefly considered taking them to the medical clinic and leaving them in the care of the midwife and the town doctor, but he dismissed the idea.

He hadn't been kidding when he said his

mother would be upset if he didn't bring Katie back. It was easier to blame her than to admit he wanted Katie and Rachel back under his roof as much as his mother did.

When Katie was settled on the seat, he handed her the baby, then picked up her suitcase and swung it into the wagon bed. After glancing around, he asked, "Where is Rachel's *babybett?*"

"I sold it," Katie answered, her voice low and filled with anguish.

"You did what?"

"I sold it to the woman who runs the Amish Trading Post to pay for my ticket but it wasn't enough. I'm so sorry. I had to do it."

And you left Rachel without a place to lay her head.

He bit back the comment he wanted to make and climbed onto the seat beside Katie. Picking up the reins with one hand, he clucked to Joey.

The big Belgian swung the wagon around and began plodding toward the edge of town. Before long, a line of cars started stacking up behind them, but he didn't care.

At the Trading Post, Elam drove into the parking lot and stopped near the front of the store. Katie withdrew a wad of bills from her pocket and silently held them out. He ignored her.

He jumped down from the wagon without saying a word and entered the building. The bassinet was on display near the counter. He picked it up, haggled the outrageous price down to one he could afford and left the store with the bed slung over his arm and his anger simmering low and hot. Outside, he climbed onto the wooden bench and set the basket between them.

As soon as Joey had them back out on the highway, Katie said. "I'm sorry. It was all I had. Please take the money."

He glanced at her from the corner of his eye. Her lips trembled pitifully. Her face was pale, her eyes red-rimmed and swollen from crying. His anger evaporated. How could he stay angry with her in the face of her obvious distress?

"Keep your money."

"But you bought back the bed."

"I bought it for Rachel, not for you. It is hers. Put your money away."

Katie extended the bills toward him. "I can't let you do that."

"Repay me by explaining why you ran off today."

Her eyes widened. She looked like a rabbit caught in the open, with nowhere to hide and a hawk swooping in for the kill.

"I wanted to reach my brother. The next bus wasn't until Monday. I didn't want to impose on you for that long."

"Since you have not given me or my mother a letter to mail to your brother, I'm going to ask why not."

She looked down at the child she held in her arms. "I have to go to Malachi in person."

"What are you not telling me, Katie Lantz?" Elam's firm tone demanded a truthful answer.

She looked away and stared at the barren fields awaiting their spring planting. "I am dead to my brother until I kneel in front of him and beg his forgiveness."

Elam could only wonder at the behavior that had forced her brother to make such a pronouncement. Church members who had committed serious offences were required to kneel in front of the congregation or the bishop and confess their sins before they could be forgiven. Her brother was not a bishop.

"Surely a letter would suffice under these circumstances," Elam said. "Had you written to him when you first came to us, you might have a reply by now."

"I wrote my brother several times in the first months after I left home. I was sorry

114

One Tree Planted for
Every Case of Paper Used

This Paper Is Sustainably Sourced
100% BPA & BPS FREE
EcoChit.com

One Tree Planted for
Every Case of Paper Used

This Paper Is Sustainably Sourced

Ramara Public Library
Brechin Branch

User name: Halliday,
Barbara M.

Title: A fatal lie [large
print]ID: 18266187
Date due: 21 January 2022
23:59
Author: Todd, Charles

Title: Katie's redemption
[large print]
Item ID: 18271689
Date due: 21 January 2022
23:59
Author: Davids, Patricia

Title: Bullseye [large print]
Item ID: 18266266
Date due: 21 January 2022
23:59
Author: Patterson, James

Total checkouts for session:
3
Total checkouts:3

To renew your items please
call 705-484-0476 or visit
ramarapubliclibrary.org
****

for the things I said and the way we parted. He sent my letters back unopened. After that, I stopped trying."

"So that's why you didn't know he had sold the farm and moved away."

"Yes."

"He will open a letter from me," Elam stated firmly.

Katie said nothing. Her eyes were closed and she swayed on the seat. She looked utterly exhausted. He said, "Why don't you put the baby in her bassinet before you drop her."

Katie's eyes shot open. "I won't drop her."

"You're both bone tired. I think she'll rest better in her bed."

"She does seem to like it. The woman at the Trading Post wanted you to make more of them."

"Is that so?" Some additional orders for his work would be welcome. He hadn't considered making baby beds. Perhaps Katie's actions would bring some good after all.

Elam let the lines go slack, but the horse continued on his way without faltering. He needed no urging to head home where there would be hay, grain and a rubdown at the end of the trip. Elam held the baby bed steady while Katie laid her daughter in it.

115

Rachel made little grunting noises as she squirmed herself into a comfortable position and drifted off to sleep.

Once he was sure she wasn't going to start fussing again, he carefully set her bed on the floorboard under the seat, where she would be out of the wind.

"She's beautiful, isn't she?" Katie asked, her voice barely audible. "I don't know what I did to deserve her."

"*Jah,* she's a right pretty baby." A baby with a young and foolish mother and a father who didn't want her. As Elam picked up the reins again, he prayed that Rachel and her mother would come to know God's love in their lives.

They rode on in silence as the last rays of sunlight cast long shadows toward the east. Elam began to make an inventory of the supplies he'd need to make more beds like the one Rachel slept in.

Suddenly, Katie slumped against Elam. He grabbed her to keep her from tumbling forward off the wagon seat and jerked Joey to a halt.

"Katie! Are you all right?"

He cupped her chin and lifted her face so he could see her. She was deathly pale. Dark circles under her eyes stood out like vivid bruises. Her eyelids fluttered open and she tried to focus on his face.

"I'm . . . so tired. . . ." Her words trailed off and her eyes closed again.

Poor thing. She was all done in. It was no wonder. She'd had a rough time of it today. He shifted his weight and settled her head against his shoulder, keeping one arm around her to hold her steady.

Elam spoke softly. "Hup now, Joey. Get along."

The horse moved forward once more. Elam tried to concentrate on the road ahead, but the feel of Katie's slender body nestled against him drove all coherent thoughts out of his head. How could something that felt so right be so wrong? She wanted no part of his faith or his way of life. He knew that, but he couldn't deny the attraction he felt for her.

He'd only held one other woman this way. Salome, the night he'd asked her to marry him. The memory of that day came rushing back.

He had nervously proposed marriage as he was driving her home in his buggy after the barn raising at Levi Knopp's farm. She'd said yes as she sat bolt upright beside him, looking straight ahead. He'd draped his arm around her shoulder wanting to hold her close.

Instantly he'd sensed her withdrawal. At the time, he put it down to her modesty and promptly withdrew his arm. It wasn't until much later that he understood she didn't return his regard. If only she'd been able to confide in him that night, a great deal of heartbreak could have been avoided.

He glanced down at Katie. She and Salome were nothing alike. Where Katie was small, slender and dark-haired, Salome had been tall, blonde and sturdy. A hardworking farm girl, she and Elam had known each other their entire lives, attending the same church and sitting on opposite sides of the one-room schoolhouse until they'd finished the eighth grade.

As with all Amish children the eighth grade was the end of their formal education. Salome had cried inconsolably the final day of school. A year later, he took her home after Sunday singing. He had only been sixteen, but he knew then that he was going to ask her to marry him someday.

Joey turned off the highway into Elam's lane and picked up the pace without urging. Katie moaned softly when the wagon wheels hit a deep rut in the dirt road.

Pushing the painful memories of Salome to the back of his mind, he again pondered Katie's situation. Why had Malachi cut her out of his life? Had it been because he felt the censure of the community over Katie's rejection of her Amish heritage? Elam found that hard to believe.

The community of Hope Springs had been welcoming and supportive. A few Amish families in the area had children who didn't follow the faith. His uncle Isaac had two children out of ten that had never been baptized. They maintained cordial relations with their parents and visited back and forth often. Uncle Isaac referred to them as his English sons. He loved and enjoyed seeing his English grandchildren.

Not all Amish felt that way. Many families simply couldn't come to terms with children who jumped the fence and never reconciled with them. Yet, for Malachi to move to another state without leaving a way for his sister to contact him spoke of a very serious breach. There had to be more to the story than Katie had told them. Perhaps his letter to Malachi would bring some answers in the return mail.

Would Katie be angry that Elam had written to her brother without her consent? He suspected she might, and that made him smile down at her. If he had learned anything about Katie Lantz, it was that she had a large measure of pride. Perhaps today's troubles had shown her the error of such thinking. Perhaps — but he doubted it.

As the wagon rolled into the farmyard, his mother rushed out of the house. "You found them. Thanks be to God. Are they all right? Where is the baby?"

"She's sleeping in her bed under the seat. Can you get her? I'm afraid to let go of Katie."

Looking up at him, Nettie seemed to notice for the first time that he had his arm around Katie. A quick frown put a crease between her brows. "Is she ill?"

"I think she's just exhausted."

Nettie stepped up to the side of the wagon and extracted the baby and her bed. "Come here, precious one. I've missed you."

Elam shook his passenger. "Katie, wake up. We're home."

"We are?" she muttered against his shoulder. Sitting up straighter, she wavered back and forth, but didn't open her eyes.

"We are. If I let go of you, will you fall off the wagon?"

It took her a long moment to reply. She pushed her hair out of her eyes and blinked hard. "I'm fine. Where's Rachel?"

"I have her," Nettie said.

Elam stepped down and held up his arms to Katie. At first he thought she intended to refuse his help, but she changed her mind. Leaning toward him, she braced her hands on his shoulders as he lifted her out of the cart.

Her knees buckled when her feet hit the ground. He scooped her up into his arms to keep her from falling.

"Put me down. I'm fine." Her slurred words and drooping eyelids said otherwise.

He shifted her higher. The feel of her slight body in his arms made him catch his breath. She was a woman who made him all too aware that he was a flesh-and-blood man. The last thing he wanted was to become involved with a woman outside his faith.

She put her arms around his neck and laid her head on his shoulder. "I said I'm fine, Elam."

She wasn't, but neither was he. Without replying, he turned and carried her into his home.

CHAPTER EIGHT

Katie woke in a familiar room. Her own room. The room she'd slept in all through her childhood. The same white-painted, unadorned walls surrounded her. The ceiling over the bed sloped low because of the roof's pitch. The series of cracks that had developed in the plaster over her head hadn't changed. When she was little, they had reminded her of stair steps leading to heaven, the place where her parents had gone.

It had been a comfort to a lonely little girl to believe that she might be able to follow them up those steps someday. Now Katie knew they were only cracks in the plaster.

She turned her head. Sunlight was streaming through the tall, narrow window because the green shade was up. It must be late.

She sat up. The room was chilly but not unbearable. The heat from the stove in the kitchen below had always kept this room warmer than any of the other upstairs bed-rooms.

She winced as she threw off the covers. Rubbing her aching arms, she quickly realized almost every part of her body throbbed with dull pain. She felt as if she'd been run over by a bus.

The bus! She'd missed the bus.

And Elam had found her weeping in the terminal parking lot.

Embarrassment flooded every fiber of her being as she recalled being carried up the narrow stairs in his arms, followed by Nettie's gentle scolding as she had readied Katie for bed.

Where was Rachel? Where was her baby?

Katie quickly checked the room, but her daughter was nowhere in sight. She noticed her suitcase beside a dark bureau along the opposite wall. Rising, she dressed quickly in a red cable-knit sweater and dark skirt, then ran her fingers through her tousled hair.

At the top of the stairs she heard women's voices. As she descended the steps, she heard laughter and banter exchanged in German. Stepping into the kitchen, she saw Nettie and three other Amish women all hard at work cleaning the room.

Nettie was the first to catch sight of Katie. "You're up. How are you feeling?" she asked in English.

Instantly, Katie found herself the focus of the other women's attention. "I'm feeling much better. Where is Rachel?"

"Elam is keeping the little ones entertained in the living room while we get our work done. Katie, these are my daughters, Ruby and Mary, and this is Ruby's sister-in-law, Sally. All of them work with Elam in his basket business."

Although farming was considered the best work, Katie knew many Amish families needed more than one income and small, home-based businesses were the norm.

Katie glanced around the room. The two women in their late twenties to early thirties were carbon copies of their mother, with blond hair, apple-red cheeks and bright blue eyes. Katie thought the youngest woman must be fifteen or sixteen. She had ginger red hair parted in the middle beneath her white *kapp* and a generous sprinkling of freckles over her upturned nose.

One of the older women stepped forward. Katie saw she was pregnant. "I'm Mary. My mother has told us about your daughter's unexpected and exciting arrival."

Mary glanced over her shoulder toward her mother then leaned closer. "I shouldn't say this, but I'm grateful you've given her something to do besides hover over me and fuss."

"I don't hover or fuss," Nettie declared.

The two sisters looked at each other and burst into giggles.

"When one of us is pregnant that's exactly what you do," Mary countered.

"*Ach,* pay them no mind, Katie. Would you like something to eat? You must be starving. You've nearly slept the clock around." Without waiting for a reply, Nettie began gathering a plate and silverware to place on the table.

Katie frowned. "I'm okay, but Rachel must be starving."

"No need to worry," Nettie answered. "I gave her some infant formula the nurse left with us. Rachel took it fine."

"I could use a bite to eat. I'm as hungry as a horse," Mary interjected.

"And as big as one," Ruby added, then ducked away from her sister's outrage.

"You just wait. Your turn will come round again, sister."

"Everyone sit down," Nettie commanded. "I have cinnamon rolls, and I can fix coffee in a jiffy."

Mary eased into a kitchen chair at the table. She looked at Katie and patted the seat beside her. "*Mamm* tells us you used to live here."

"I did. My mother died in a fire when I was just a toddler. My brother Malachi and his wife took me in. This was his house."

Before Katie sat down to eat she had to check on Rachel. She moved to the living room doorway. Looking in, she saw Elam with the baby in his arms and three little boys playing with blocks around his feet. Elam hadn't noticed her as he was trying to keep the oldest boys from squabbling over the ownership of a carved wooden horse.

Her daughter looked so tiny balanced against his broad chest. For Katie, it was odd to see a man who wasn't intimidated by a newborn baby. Elam firmly but kindly settled the brewing quarrel and sat back in his chair to keep a watchful eye on the bunch. Rachel looked quite content where she was, so Katie returned to the table and sat down.

She was hungry so she made short work of the delicious cinnamon bun and the glass of milk Nettie placed in front of her.

While Mary and Ruby seemed at ease with their mother's houseguest, Sally remained quiet. She had a hard time meeting Katie's eyes. The young Amish girl obviously hadn't had much exposure to the English or an ex-Amish who was trying to be English.

Finally, Sally worked up the nerve to speak. "Did you really live in Cincinnati? What was it like in such a big city?"

How do I answer that question? My experience was colored by so many different things, Katie thought.

She smiled at Sally. "When I first moved there it was very exciting. Especially at night. You can't imagine the lights. They glow from every tall building and many stay on all night long."

"It sounds so exciting." Sally's tone was wistful.

Katie knew just how it felt to wonder about forbidden things so far away. "Although it can be pretty, it was also terrifying. It was far, far different than I imagined."

Sally leaned forward eagerly. "Are you going back there?"

"I'm not sure what I'm going to do."

"I would like to see the city. My *dat* sometimes travels there for his furniture business, but he's never taken me. Are the buildings really so tall that they block out the sun?"

"It's a place filled with wickedness ready to ensnare the unwary." Elam spoke from the doorway to the living room. He still held

Rachel in his arms.

Katie felt the heat rising in her cheeks. He was talking about her. She raised her chin, refusing to give in to the need to keep her head down. Amazed at her own daring, she replied, "Wickedness can ensnare the unwary no matter where they are. Even on the family farm."

He met her gaze, then nodded slightly. "That is true."

An awkward silence ensued until Sally asked, "Elam, my *dat* wants to know when you need me to start weaving again."

"I'll be ready to start the middle of next week, if that's okay with everyone."

All the women nodded. One of the boys, the littlest one, who looked to be about a year old, crawled over to Elam's leg and pulled himself upright and babbled away. Elam reached down to steady the child. "Monroe thinks he is hungry, Ruby."

Nettie came and took the boy from him. His older brother wriggled between Elam's leg and the doorjamb. "I'm starving, *Mamm.*"

"You don't fool me, Thomas. You heard the words *cinnamon roll.*"

A wide grin split his cheeks, and he bobbed his blond head.

Elam rubbed his stomach. "I'm hungry,

too. It's hard work watching the children. I've worked up an appetite."

Ruby threw up her hands. "That's what I tell my Jesse, but he doesn't believe me."

A shout from outside drew everyone's attention. Elam looked out the window. "The bench wagon is here."

Nettie, dishing out rolls to each of the women at the table and their assorted children, said, "Oh, my, and I'm not done with the cleaning."

Katie realized the arrival of the bench wagon meant that the family was making preparations for the *Gemeesunndaag,* the church Sunday, to be held in their home.

The Amish had no formal house of worship. Instead, a preaching service was held every other Sunday in the home of one church family. Up to a hundred and twenty people had attended services in the house when Katie was growing up. In fact, the wall between the kitchen and the living room was constructed so that it could be moved aside to make more space for the benches that were lined up for the men on one side and the women on the other.

In their district, the church owned the benches required to seat so many people and transported them from home to home for each service as they were needed. In the summertime, church was occasionally held in the cool interiors of large barns in the area.

"I'll have the men stack the benches on the porch." Elam approached Katie and handed over the baby. She took care not to touch him, as her heart skipped a beat and then raced ahead of her good sense at his nearness. When he was close, the memory of his strong arms around her brought the heat of a blush rushing to her face. She glanced around covertly, hoping no one noticed her reaction.

There was something about Elam that stirred feelings she didn't want to acknowledge. What a fickle woman she must be. Once she'd imagined herself in love with Matt. Now she was wrestling with those same emotions when Elam was near.

No. These were not the same emotions.

Elam was kindness and charity. He was strength and faith. He was as different from Matt as day was from night.

How had she been fooled into thinking that what she felt for Matt was love? It had been a shallow substitute. She understood that now. Why hadn't she been smart enough to see it before she'd made such a mess of her life?

With her daughter in her arms, Katie rose,

wanting to escape the turmoil of her own thoughts. "I'll feed Rachel and then I'll be back to help you get ready for church."

Nettie shook her head. "We can do this. You need to rest."

"I've already slept the clock around. How much more rest do I need?" Katie countered.

"A lot. You go take it easy," Ruby said, gathering up the plates.

What Katie really wanted to do was race up to her room and hide under the warm quilt on her bed. It would have been easy to withdraw and hide, but she couldn't do it. She wanted to earn the respect this family was showing her. And she wanted to show Elam that she was more than a helpless, sobbing woman in need of rescue.

Elam escaped outside and drew a deep breath — one filled with the smell of a muddy farmyard, not with the sweet, womanly scent that was so uniquely Katie's.

What was wrong with him? Why did his thoughts continually turn to her? The memory of carrying her in his arms had haunted him long into the night and came rushing back the moment he'd seen her today.

Was he so weak in his faith that he was

only attracted to the forbidden fruit? Katie had chosen to be an outsider. He should have nothing to do with her.

Be ye not unequally yoked together with unbelievers: for what fellowship hath righteousness with unrighteousness? and what communion hath light with darkness?

The Plain people were to live apart from the world. He must harden his heart against Katie's dark eyes so full of pain and loneliness. He had to resist the need to make her smile. To touch her soft skin, to kiss her full lips. She was not for him.

Eli Imhoff stepped down from the bench wagon. "*Goot* day, Elam. Jacob and I have brought the benches for your house."

"*Danki,* Mr. Imhoff, and my thanks to you, as well, Jacob." Elam nodded to the teenage boy sitting on the back of the wagon.

The boy nodded and held out a bundle of letters and the newspaper. "The mailman was dropping this off as we came by. I thought I'd save you a trip down the lane."

"*Danki,* Jacob." Elam took the mail and laid it on his mother's rocker near the front door.

Walking to the back of the wagon, Mr. Imhoff lowered the tailgate. "Shall we get started?"

Elam hurried to join them. "*Jah,* and then

you must stay for a cup of coffee. My mother has just made some."

Mr. Imhoff, a widower, glanced toward the house. "How is your mother getting along? Is she liking Hope Springs?"

Perhaps it was his awareness of Katie's effect on him that made Elam notice the odd quality in Mr. Imhoff's simple questions.

"Mother is well. She misses her friends back home, but I think she likes the area well enough."

"*Goot.* Very *goot.*" Mr. Imhoff grinned and began pulling off the first seat. After unloading the sturdy wooden benches and stacking them together on the porch, Elam invited Mr. Imhoff and his son into the house.

Elam picked up the mail as he followed them inside. He laid the letters on the counter, more interested in the looks and shy smiles that passed between his neighbor and his mother. How long had this been going on? His mother had been a widow for three years now, but he'd never considered that she might be interested in another man.

After accepting a cup of coffee, Mr. Imhoff said, "I was just asking your son if you're adjusting to our community."

"I find it much to my liking, especially

since two of my daughters and my son are here."

"It's a blessing to have your family close by." Mr. Imhoff blew on his coffee to cool it.

Jacob was drawn into the other room by Elam's nephews. The next time Elam glanced that way, the strapping boy was down on the floor with them. Mr. Imhoff followed Elam's gaze. "He's used to having little ones underfoot."

The sound of someone descending the stairs made Elam tense. He hadn't thought of how he would introduce Katie to the members of his church.

She came through the door holding Rachel on her shoulder. Her English clothing and uncovered head made her stand out in the room filled with Plain women. She nodded politely at the visitors.

Elam's mother stepped in to fill the awkward silence. "This is our visitor. Mr. Imhoff, perhaps you remember Katie Lantz."

He nodded in her direction. "Quiet little Katie with the dark eyes? I do, but you are much changed. How is your brother? Is he happy in Kansas? My cousin moved there a few years ago. He says a man can own land and not farm it, but make a living by renting his grass out for other men's cows to

134

graze on."

"I have not seen my brother in quite a while," Katie admitted.

"I'm sorry to hear that. Family is so very important."

Katie looked lovingly at the child she held. "I'm beginning to understand that."

Mr. Imhoff sighed. "I wish God had seen fit to leave mine with me longer."

Nettie laid a hand on his arm. "We take comfort in knowing they are with God."

He patted her hand, allowing his fingers to linger on hers longer than Elam thought necessary.

Elam knew that Mr. Imhoff's wife and three of his seven children had been killed when a car struck their buggy several years ago. His oldest daughter, Karen, had taken over the reins of the family and was raising her younger siblings.

Nettie caught her son looking her way and withdrew her hand. Mr. Imhoff said quickly, "My daughter wants you to know she'll be happy to help with the meal and the cleanup after church if you wish it."

Nettie cast a sly look at Elam before she replied. "Tell Karen her help will be most welcome."

Even his sisters exchanged speaking looks and little smiles. Mary said, "*Jah,* we always welcome Karen's help."

A possible reason for their covert glances suddenly dawned on him. Karen was single and close to his own age. Had the women of his family decided on some matchmaking?

Shaking his head, he turned away and picked up the mail. Sorting through it, he froze when his glance fell on a long white envelope. The return address was Yoder, Kansas. It was an answer from Malachi Lantz.

Elam's heart dropped to his boots. He glanced to where Katie was happily showing her daughter to Mr. Imhoff.

Her brother had written. That meant she would be leaving soon.

Elam leaned back against the counter. That was what he wanted, wasn't it? So why wasn't he glad?

CHAPTER NINE

When Mr. Imhoff and his son left, Katie excused herself from the group in the kitchen and carried Rachel into the living room where the bassinet was set up. When Katie attempted to put her down, her daughter displayed an unusual streak of bad temper and threw a fit. The young boys were immediately intrigued by the baby and crowded around, their toys forgotten.

"Why is she crying?" the older boy asked in Pennsylvania Dutch. He, like all Amish children, would not learn more than a few words of English until he started school.

She answered him in kind. "I think she is tired, but she's afraid she'll miss something interesting if she goes to sleep."

"Can I hold her?"

"If you sit quietly on the sofa, you may."

The boys scrambled onto the couch and sat up straight. Katie laid Rachel in Thomas's arms. The baby immediately fell silent as she focused on the unfamiliar face. The difference between her dark-haired baby and the boys with their white-blond hair was striking.

Thomas grinned at Katie. "She likes me."

Katie smiled back at him. "I think she does."

She was sitting beside Thomas showing him how to support Rachel's head, when Elam came into the room. Katie looked up and froze when she saw the expression on his face. He drew a chair close and sat in front of her.

He glanced at the boys. "Thomas, I need someone to gather the eggs today. Can you boys do that?"

Thomas puffed up. "Sure."

Katie took Rachel from the boy. Clearly Elam wanted to talk to her without the children in the room. A sense of unease settled in the pit of her stomach.

"*Gut.* Get a basket for the eggs from your grandmother." Elam ruffled Thomas's hair. The boy hurried to do the chore with his younger cousin following close behind.

Katie held Rachel and rocked her gently, waiting for Elam to speak.

"I wrote to your brother shortly after you came to us."

Her heart sank. "You did what?"

"It was clear you couldn't find the words. I did not tell him anything about Rachel. I only said that you were staying with us, but had not the means to get to Kansas."

"I wish you hadn't done that, Elam."

"I know. I'm sorry I didn't tell you sooner." After a moment, he held out a white envelope. "This came this morning."

Katie tried to hide her trepidation, but she could feel Elam's gaze on her as she stared at the envelope without moving. She asked, "What does he say?"

"I haven't opened it. I thought perhaps you would like to do that."

"It's addressed to you. You should read it." She lifted her chin, expecting the worst but praying for the best.

"All right."

She struggled to maintain a brave front. He tore open the envelope and read the short note inside.

His expression hardened. He pressed his lips together.

"Well?" Katie asked.

He read aloud. " 'Dear Mr. Sutter, I am sorry to hear Katie has burdened your family with her presence. Please understand it is with a heavy heart that I tell you she is not welcome in our home.' "

Elam stopped reading to look at her.

"Perhaps it would be better if you read the rest in private."

She shook her head and clutched Rachel more tightly. "No, go on."

Swallowing hard, Elam resumed reading. " 'I will not make arrangements for Katie to travel here. Beware of her serpent's tongue. She has fooled us too often with her words of repentance uttered in falsehood. I pray God will take pity on her soul. She is no longer kin of mine. Your friend in Christ, Malachi Lantz.' "

Katie cringed as Elam lowered the letter. Though she had tried to prepare herself for Malachi's response, it still hurt. She turned her face away as tears stung her eyes.

She was disgraced with nowhere to go. All her struggles to reach her family had been in vain.

Looking into Elam's sympathetic eyes, she said, "I had hoped Malachi would take us in, but if he has publicly disowned me . . . he won't. I did not believe he would do this."

"Perhaps when he learns you have a child."

She shook her head. "I don't see how that will make him think better of me."

"What about Matt's family?"

"I never met any of them. I think Matt

was too ashamed of me."

"Ashamed or not, he has a duty to provide for his child."

"I don't know how to reach him or his family. Mrs. Zimmerman said they were out of the country."

Katie looked up at Elam through her tears. "I truly had nowhere to go."

Elam longed to gather her into his arms and comfort her, but he couldn't. It wouldn't be right. How could a brother be so cold-hearted? And Matt! To cast aside a woman and ignore his own child. What kind of man could do that? Elam wanted to shake them both.

Now was the time for her family to show Katie compassion, to welcome her back as the prodigal child and show her the true meaning of Christian forgiveness.

While he had no way of knowing what had transpired between the siblings before Katie left home, this didn't seem right. Many young people made mistakes and fell away from the true path during their *rumspringa,* the "running around" time of adolescents, but it was unusual for a person to be disowned by their family because of such activity.

Elam stared at Katie, trying to see her as

her brother saw her. Tears stained her cheeks. She couldn't disguise the hurt in her eyes. She was simply a young woman struggling to find her way in life.

"Is what your brother said true?"

"About my serpent's tongue? Maybe it is. I was ready to pretend to be Amish again so that Rachel and I would have somewhere to live."

"So you were going to lie to your brother when you faced him."

"I don't know what I would have done. I was so desperate."

Would she have lied? Elam wanted to believe she would have found the strength to tell the truth. "What will you do now?"

"I'll find work. I'll take care of Rachel."

"What if you can't find work?"

She managed a crooked half smile. "I have a little money put back that I won't have to use on a bus ticket. If I can't find work here, then I'll go to the next town and the next one until I do find something."

"You can't wander the country with a baby."

She shot to her feet. "I'll do whatever I have to do to take care of my child."

Elam stared at her dumbfounded as she stormed out of the room and up the stairs.

A few minutes later, his mother came in

the room and began picking up toys. "Your sisters are leaving. Ruby has some baby clothes for little Rachel. I thought Katie was in here? Where did she go?"

Elam held up Malachi's letter. "I heard from her brother today."

Nettie's happy smile faded. "Oh. I knew she wouldn't be with us long, but I had hoped she could stay a few more days. I've grown so fond of her and of that baby. How soon is Malachi coming?"

"He's not."

"What?"

"He says that she is no longer kin of his."

"That's ridiculous."

Elam held out the paper. "Read for yourself."

Taking the note, Nettie settled herself in the chair beside him and adjusted her glasses. After reading the short missive she handed it back. "Well, I never. His own sister is destitute and begging for his help and he is refusing to acknowledge her. No wonder *Gott* sent that child to us."

"Her brother may have his reasons. We can't know his heart, only God can."

"You think this is right?"

"No, but what we think isn't important."

Nettie stood. "She is going to need friends now that she has no family."

His mind told him he could be a friend to Katie, but he realized in his heart he wanted to be much more. Unless she gave up her English ways, that would never happen.

Sunday morning dawned overcast and gray. The warm spell had come to an end. Winter reclaimed the land for a little while longer, sending a cold, drizzling rain that fit Katie's mood. She would have to make some kind of decision soon. Without her brother, she had no one to turn to now. She needed a new plan.

As much as she wanted to be angry with Malachi, she couldn't. She'd never felt like she belonged in his home.

Gazing at her baby sleeping sweetly in her arms, Katie tried to block out the despair that threatened to overwhelm her. She was bone tired. Between Rachel's frequent night feedings and the lingering effects of her hike into town, she could barely keep her eyes open. Any sleep she did get was filled with nightmares of what would happen to them now. No matter what, she had to protect her child.

Outside, buggy after buggy began to arrive. Katie watched the gathering from her upstairs window. Families came together, the men and boys in their black suits and hats, the girls and women in dark dresses with their best black bonnets on their heads.

While most came in buggies, a number of people arrived on foot. Before long the yard was filled with black buggies and the line stretched partway down the lane. The tired horses, some who'd brought a family from as far away as fifteen miles, were unhitched and taken to the corrals.

Nettie had invited Katie to attend services, but she had declined. She didn't belong among them. She didn't belong anywhere.

What was she going to do? How would she take care of Rachel? How would they live?

Why had God sent her this trial?

She turned her limited options over and over in her mind. Perhaps Amber had learned of a job Katie could take? It didn't matter what it was. She'd do anything. Anything.

She turned away from the window. Knowing that the services would last for several hours, she was prepared to stay in her room the entire time. What she wasn't prepared for was the tug of emotion she felt when the first familiar hymn began.

Downstairs, the slow and mournful chanting rose in volume, as voices blended together in one of the ancient songs that had been passed down through the generations. No music accompanied the singing. The Amish needed only the voices of the faithful.

Listening to the words of sorrow, hope and God's promise of salvation, Katie felt a stirring deep within her soul. She knew sorrow, she needed hope, but she was afraid to trust God's mercy.

Moving to the door, Katie opened it a crack. The song continued for another few minutes, then silence fell over the house. She opened the door farther and caught the sound of a man's voice. The preaching had begun, but she couldn't quite make out the words.

Moving outside her room, she stopped at the top of the stairwell where she could hear better. Standing soon grew tiring and she sank down to sit on the top riser.

Cuddling Rachel close to her heart, Katie closed her eyes and listened to the words of the preacher. The scripture readings and preaching were in German, but she had no trouble understanding them.

When the second hymn began, Katie found herself softly singing along as she pondered the meaning of the words for her own life.

When the three-hour service concluded,

she heard the rustling of people rising and the flow of social talk getting underway. Shortly, the gathering meal would start.

Suddenly, an Amish woman started up the stairs. When she looked up, Katie recognized Sally.

The young woman stopped a few steps below Katie. "Nettie says you have to eat and it's time to come down. She won't take no for an answer."

Nodding, Katie rose. It was time to face the community she had turned her back on.

She had no illusions that everyone would be as welcoming as Elam and his mother had been. Drawing a deep breath, she descended the stairs with Rachel in her arms.

When she came out of the stairway, she saw Elam off to one side of the room with several other men who were rearranging the benches and forming tables by stacking them together. Not knowing what to do, Katie simply stood out of the way.

It wasn't long before Nettie caught sight of her. "Katie, come help me set the tables."

Sally returned to Katie's side and reached for Rachel. "I'll take her."

Handing over her daughter, Katie smiled at Sally. "Thanks."

Now that she had two free hands, Katie

joined Nettie and her daughters in the kitchen. Other women came in carrying hampers laden with fresh breads, meat pies, homemade butter and jams as well as cheeses. Many covert glances came Katie's way, but no one made comments.

Katie and Ruby began setting a knife, cup and saucer at each place around the tables. Since there wasn't enough room to feed everyone at once, the ordained and eldest church members would eat first. The youngest among them would have to wait until last.

Katie was amazed at how natural it felt to be doing such an ordinary task with Nettie and her family. No one chided her or scolded her for sloppy work. She laughed in response to some story Ruby relayed about her boys. Looking across the room, she met Elam's gaze. He gave her a small smile and a nod. She felt the color rush to her cheeks, but she smiled back.

Looking down, she laid another knife by a cup and saucer. She could almost pretend this was her family and this was where she belonged.

When she looked up again, Elam stood across the table from her. He said, "It is good you're not hiding anymore."

She glanced toward the women gathering

in the kitchen. "I'm not sure the worst is over."

"I pray that it is, Katie." It seemed as if he wanted to say more, but he didn't.

She watched as he went out to the barn to wait his turn to eat with the other young men. She couldn't help but wonder how he would explain her presence to his friends.

Elam stood just inside the wide-open barn doors amid a group of ten other young men near his age. He was the only clean-shaven one in the group. They were all farmers and his neighbors, and all were married with growing families. A number of those children raced by playing a game of hide-and-seek in the barn. The dreary weather hadn't put a damper on the jovial mood of those around Elam.

"Heard you planned on planting pumpkins this year," Aaron Zook remarked. The bishop's son farmed sixty acres across the road from Elam's place.

Aaron had been the one to help Elam develop the area's newly formed organic food cooperative. Limited to small acreages by their reliance on horses, the local Amish farmers had been struggling to compete with the commercial produce farms in the area. But thanks to Aaron and Elam's efforts, they were finding a niche in a new, fast-growing market as certified organic farmers.

"Prices aren't what they were last year," Samuel Stutzman cautioned.

Elam fought back a smile. Samuel always thought last year's prices were better. "I'm going to try a small field of pumpkins. They're a good fall cash crop, but mostly I'll be sticking to cabbage, potatoes and onions."

Aaron pushed aside his black coat to hook his thumbs in his suspenders. "I'm going to plant more watermelon and cantaloupe. They did the best for me."

Elam kept one ear in the conversation, but planting and cash crops weren't what was foremost on his mind. He looked past the array of black coats, beards and black hats to the house. He had no trouble picking Katie out among the throngs of women on the porch waiting their turn to eat. Her simple gray skirt and red sweater made her stand out like a sore thumb. The women of his family surrounded her.

They were making it plain that Katie was a friend and accepted by them. Part of him was proud of their actions, but another part feared their public display of support would bring disapproval down on them. Katie's history would keep many of the women from acknowledging her.

His mother was talking to Karen Imhoff. Karen's father, rather than gathering with the men, was helping move the tables where Elam's mother directed him.

"Elam, might I have a word with you?"

He turned to find Bishop Zook at his elbow. "Of course, Bishop."

"Come. Walk with me."

CHAPTER TEN

Elam walked silently alongside the bishop until they were out of earshot from the men in the barn.

The bishop spoke at last. "I see that Katie Lantz is still with you."

"*Jah.* She missed the bus."

"I had hoped to hear she was turning from her English ways?"

"Not yet, but my mother is a good influence on her."

"Let us pray so." He took a deep breath and then continued. "There has been talk, Elam. I tell you this because I value you as a member of the church. You have done much to preserve our way of life."

"I can assure you that nothing unacceptable has happened in my home."

The bishop stopped walking and turned to face him. "I believe you. You are an upright man, but such talk can take on a life of its own. Some are saying that your family cares more about outsiders than our own people."

Anger rose up in Elam, but he worked to suppress it. "Because of my father?"

"Word has reached us of your troubles back in Pennsylvania. Perhaps that is why members of the district have scrutinized you so closely. Taking in this woman wasn't a good idea. We must limit our contact with those who do not believe as we do."

"What would you have me do? Turn her and her child out to beg on the roadside?"

"Of course not, but surely you could arrange for her to travel to her brother's home."

"He has disowned her. The baby's father has abandoned her. She has nowhere to go."

The bishop frowned as he rubbed his neck. "Malachi has disowned his own sister? I had not heard this."

"The letter came yesterday. My mother is only doing her Christian duty in caring for Katie and her baby. Perhaps you can stem this gossip."

"I will do what I can, but I can only do so much."

Elam nodded, but his frustration boiled beneath the surface. It was so unfair. He hadn't lived a blameless life, but he had always loved his faith and tried to do God's will. His mother was a good and kind woman. That should not be held against her.

The bishop began walking back toward the house. "If Katie's brother would change his mind it might solve this problem."

"She does not believe he will. From the tone of his letter, I fear she is right."

"I will write to Malachi and the bishop of his district and explain the situation. Perhaps Malachi can be persuaded to listen to wiser counsel. So you are thinking of planting pumpkins. I've been considering that myself."

Elam followed the bishop's lead and changed the subject back to spring planting.

As they walked back to the gathering, Elam related what he knew about the new variety of pumpkins available, but inside he was deeply worried.

He would not turn Katie and Rachel out of his home, but neither could he stand by and watch his family be shunned again.

Katie was acutely aware that she was the focus of much speculation among the district members. A few of the younger women, friends of Mary and Ruby, came up to be introduced. Some of them Katie remembered from her school days. For the most part, the older women of the group ignored her. Katie recognized many of them as friends of her sister-in-law, Beatrice.

From the covert glances cast her way, she knew most, if not all, were aware that she was an unwed mother.

Another poor Amish girl come to no good in the English world. They would point her out to their teenage daughters as an example of why English men weren't to be trusted.

She glanced toward Elam. Did he see her as spoiled goods?

As she watched, Bishop Zook left Elam's side and came toward her. The bishop looked pensive, but Elam had a deep scowl on his face. Apprehension crawled across her skin.

She folded her hands and lowered her gaze. "Hello, Bishop Zook."

"Hello, Katie. It's been a long time."

"Yes, it has."

"Might I have a word with you in private?"

"Of course." She folded her arms to keep her hands from trembling.

They left the porch and walked to where a large oak tree provided some shelter from the light mist.

"I'm sorry to hear of your troubles. What are your plans now that you are back in Hope Springs?"

"I will be looking for work."

"I see. It won't be easy with a new baby to take care of."

Katie glanced toward the house. "Life is not meant to be easy. That is why we pray for God's strength to help us bear it."

"That is true."

She studied Bishop Zook's lined face and saw only kind concern. His long gray beard was considered a sign of wisdom. She hoped that was true. "Is my presence causing trouble for the Sutters?"

"You wish to protect them?"

"I would not hurt them for the world."

"Let me ask you this. Do you plan to join the church?"

If she gave the bishop that impression, would it prevent the censure of Elam and his family? She didn't want to lie. She chose a middle ground and hoped it would be enough.

"I have been gone a long time. I need to reaccustom myself to the community before making a decision. Joining the church is not a step to be taken lightly."

He rocked back on his heels. "That is wise. Since you were not a member when you left, you will not be expected to make a confession to the church should you decide to begin instructions for baptism. Don't hesitate to come to me if you feel you are in need of guidance."

Relief swept over her. She had bought herself more time without an outright lie. "I will keep that in mind."

As the bishop walked away, Katie headed back to the house. She reached the steps just as Mrs. Zook and several women came out after having finished their meal. The stark expressions on their faces sent a bolt of apprehension through Katie.

Lifting her chin a notch, Katie nodded toward the bishop's wife. "Good day, Mrs. Zook."

She didn't reply. She and the other women turned their faces aside. The brims of their black bonnets effectively blocking their faces from Katie's view as they walked past her without a word.

Katie's smile slipped as humiliation drained the blood from her face. She could feel the eyes of everyone watching her. Glancing across the yard, she saw Elam staring at her. He stood without moving for a long moment, then he turned away. Her whole body started shaking.

A second later, Nettie was at her side. "Sally says that Rachel is getting fussy. Why don't you take her upstairs and I'll bring you something to eat."

157

Grateful for Nettie's quick intervention, Katie tried to smile, but her throat ached with unshed tears. She quickly fled into the house where Sally was watching Rachel in Nettie's room.

"I tell you, Elam, I was shocked. The bishop's wife snubbed Katie in front of everyone."

Sitting in his living room that evening, Elam pondered what to tell his mother about his conversation with the bishop. He glanced at the ceiling. Katie had gone to her room and hadn't come down.

Sighing deeply, he said, "The bishop told me talk is already circulating in the community. Some people are saying we are going against the *Ordnung* by allowing Katie to stay here."

"Are you worried about a few gossips who have nothing better to do? And the bishop's wife is the worst offender."

"Which means her words will carry much weight with him. You must take care."

"Are you trying to protect me or yourself? Search your heart, Elam. Katie is a lost sheep, but she wants to find her way back to God."

"I have not heard her say this."

"That's because you aren't listening. We

must be a light for her, Elam. We can show her God's goodness and His kindness. If we send her away, we only prove that she doesn't belong here. That child wants so much to belong somewhere. She has been made to feel apart her whole life. Her heart is crying out for someone to care about her, but she is afraid."

"Afraid of what?"

"She's afraid of the same thing that frightens you. She's afraid that she doesn't deserve to be happy."

"I'm not afraid."

She took his hands between her own. "I know your heart has been broken. I know your trust was betrayed. None of it was your fault, Elam. You must forgive."

"I have."

"You say that, but I think there is still bitterness in your heart."

There was, and he hated himself for it. "Have you forgotten how much we all suffered when we had to shun *Dat?* How we begged and pleaded with him to come back to God? Do you remember how your friends stopped seeing you? Of standing on the porch and hearing Deacon Hertzler tell both of you that you were excommunicated because you could not bear to shun your own husband. I heard your weeping, *Mamm,* night after night."

"I have not forgotten, Elam," she answered quietly. "But I made my confession, and I was welcomed back into the church after your father died."

He struggled to bring his agitation under control. "But it was never the same. It must be different here or we have uprooted our lives for nothing."

"And Katie? What part did she play in those sorrows?"

The breath whooshed out of his lungs. He hung his head. "None."

"She has been abandoned by everyone she loved. You and I, we know the pain of that. Of trusting and loving someone only to find that love isn't enough."

"What would you have me do?"

"I would have you show her the compassion I know lives in your heart."

CHAPTER ELEVEN

"What will you do now?" Nettie hung a pair of Elam's pants on the clothesline and secured them with wooden clothespins. Monday was wash day.

Beside her, Katie hung up one of Rachel's gowns and reached into the basket for another. "I can't continue living on your charity."

"Don't worry about that," Nettie mumbled around the clothespin she held in her mouth. She secured another pair of pants and said, "You've been a help to me. My wash is going twice as easy with your help."

Katie rolled her eyes. "You could do Monday wash with one hand tied behind your back."

Chuckling, Nettie said, "I've done it with one toddler on my hip and two at my ankles, but I appreciate your help anyway. I'm not as young as I used to be."

Picking up a pair of her own slacks, Katie said, "All I've done is add to your work."

"Your few pants and blouses add very little to my workload. You need more clothes."

Katie was thankful she had packed a few of her pre-pregnancy outfits in her suitcase. "If I keep eating your good cooking, I'm going to have to start wearing my maternity pants again."

"You don't eat enough to make a mouse fat. I would loan you some of my dresses, but they'd be much too big. You are welcome to borrow some things from my daughters. Mary will be happy to loan you a few dresses. The two of you are about the same size."

She'd sworn she would never wear Plain clothes again. After shaking the wrinkles out of one of Nettie's navy dresses, Katie pinned it to the line. The simple designs and solid colors didn't seem as restrictive as she'd once thought them. Wearing sweatshirts and jeans hadn't made her happy or made her feel she belonged in the English world.

She picked up a white sheet. Tossing it over the cord, she adjusted it until it hung evenly. The wind that set it to flapping was cold. The sun played peekaboo behind low gray clouds.

Securing the sheet, Katie said, "Thanks for the offer, but what I need is to get a job. Then I can buy my own clothes and pay rent on my own place."

"Who will take care of Rachel while you work?"

"I'll find someone. There must be a day-care center in Hope Springs."

"It's not right to let others raise your child."

Katie sighed. "What choice do I have?"

"Perhaps your brother will reconsider." Elam's deep voice startled Katie and she nearly dropped the pillowcase she was holding.

Why did he have such an effect on her? She took a deep breath to quiet her rapid pulse. "He might if I go to him in person."

"And if he won't take you in, then you've gone all the way to Kansas for no reason and you'll be worse off than you are now because you'll not have a single friend there." Nettie scowled at her son.

Nettie pulled a shirt from the laundry basket at her feet and shook it vigorously. "What your brother needs is a serious attitude adjustment!"

Katie's mouth fell open. She looked at Elam and they both started laughing. He said, "*Mamm,* where did you hear such talk?"

Her gaze darted between their startled faces. "I heard Jacob Imhoff say it about his little brother. Why? Doesn't it mean he must change his mind?"

Smiling at her, Katie said, "It means you'd like someone to beat him up and change his mind for him."

Taken aback, Nettie raised her eyebrows. "Is that what Jacob meant? Well, I hope and pray your brother finds it in his heart to offer you aid, but I certainly don't wish him harm."

Neither did Katie. With her limited options, she knew she needed to find work as soon as possible. "Would it be all right if I borrowed the buggy this afternoon?"

Elam nodded. "I won't be using it."

"I'd like to see if I can find work in town."

"I will drive you." Elam started to leave.

Katie stopped him by saying, "I can drive myself. I've not been among the English so long that I've forgotten how to handle a buggy."

He scowled at her. "Very well. Have it your way. What time will you be wanting to leave?"

She gestured toward the baskets of laundry waiting to be hung on the clotheslines.

"As soon as we are done here."

"Then I'll get Judy hitched up now."

As he strode away, Katie said, "I'm sorry if I made him angry."

"He doesn't know how to handle a woman who wants to make her own way in life."

"I've spent my whole life waiting for a man to take care of me. I thought that was the way it should be, but if I hadn't been so dependent on Matt, and on my brother before that, I wouldn't be in this situation. I'm not going to blithely put my life in the hands of another man. I'm going to take care of myself and I'm going to take care of Rachel."

"I believe you will," Nettie said.

Katie's irritation faded. "It's just bold talk. I haven't a clue how to take care of myself or a baby. Nettie, what am I going to do?"

"Pray to God for guidance and take things one day at a time."

One day at a time. Nettie's advice repeated itself over and over in Katie's mind as she drove toward Hope Springs an hour later. There was little else she could do.

On Main Street, people turned to stare as she drove past. A woman dressed in a red plaid coat and blue jeans driving an Amish buggy was an odd sight to say the least.

At the Trading Post, the same woman that

had bought Elam's bassinet was rearranging items on a clearance rack. She looked up at the sound of the bell over the door. "Welcome to the Trading Post. Is there something I can help you with? Oh, you're the young woman who came in with that adorable little bassinet. I sold it the very same day. I don't suppose you've brought more, have you?"

Katie decided not to tell her she'd sold it to the man who made it. "Actually, I've come looking for a job."

"I'm sorry. We aren't hiring now, but we usually take on summer help starting about mid-May. If you want, I can give you an application."

Hiding her disappointment, Katie said, "That would be great."

"I'm sure I can sell more of those baby carriers."

"I'll tell the man who made mine." Katie filled out the application and left it with the woman, but the idea of waiting another month and a half for a job was discouraging.

The responses at the other merchants and eateries in town were pretty much the same. No one needed help, but most said they would be hiring when the tourist season got underway.

166

Dejected, Katie left a half-dozen applications with various merchants and turned Judy toward home.

Katie was unhitching the horse when Elam appeared at her side. He said, "Let me give you a hand with that."

"I can manage."

"I know you can, but I'm going to help anyway." He took the heavy harness out of her hands. "How did your job hunting go?"

"Not well. You may be stuck with me until the tourists arrive."

"I thought as much."

Katie pulled off Judy's headstall and paused to draw her hand down the horse's silky black neck. Unlike her brother and some Amish, Katie knew Elam took good care of his horses. He was kind to animals and stray women. She shouldn't read anything into the way he'd cared for her and her baby. "I'm sorry, Elam. If I didn't have Rachel, I'd just go, but I have to think of her welfare."

"You are being foolish to worry about this. God will provide."

"He hasn't done such a good job so far."

"Do not mock Him. He brought you to my mother, didn't He? What better care could He have provided than that?"

"I'm sorry. I'm just frustrated and angry."

167

"Angry about what?"

"Everything. I'm angry with Matt for leaving me. I'm angry with my brother for disowning me. I'm angry at the people in town who don't need help until summer."

"Are you angry with me?"

She turned to face him. "Of course not. You and your mother have been kindness itself."

"But you still wish to leave and go back among the English."

Did she? There were times when her previous life seemed like an unreal dream. She hadn't truly been happy on this farm, but she hadn't been happy in the city, either. What was wrong with her? What was missing inside her that made her feel she was always on the outside looking in?

Katie led Judy into her stall, turned the mare loose and closed the gate. Facing Elam, Katie knew only the truth would satisfy him.

"I don't belong here, Elam. I never fit in, not with my family, not with the other Amish kids. I was always different. Sometimes I used to wonder if I'd ever find a place where I did belong."

"Would staying here really be so bad?" he asked softly.

Did she imagine the soft pleading in his

voice? She must have. It was only wishful thinking on her part. He had no interest in her as a woman. She wasn't of his faith. It was foolish to consider there could be anything between them.

Katie moved to hang up the harness, needing to put some distance between herself and the man who disturbed her peace of mind. She needed to get a handle on her wayward emotions. "I don't want to be a burden on anyone. I need to make a life of my own. To do that, I must find work."

He was silent for so long that she thought he'd gone. When she turned around, he was standing with his hands in his pockets and his head bowed.

Finally, he said, "I've been thinking of hiring more help for my woodshop. I've been getting a fair number of orders for my baskets. More than I'll be able to fill once spring planting starts. Ruby, Mary and Sally all work with me in the business."

"Why haven't I seen them working?"

"I've been remodeling my workroom, but it's done now. They'll all be back to work the day after tomorrow. Of course, once Mary has her baby she'll be at home, but by then you should be able to pick up her slack. Would you be interested in work like that?"

Katie couldn't believe her ears. "Are you offering me a job?"

"You will get paid a commission for each piece you make. It won't be much to start with. Not like the jobs you could get in Cincinnati."

"A woman with nothing but an eighth grade education doesn't earn much, even if she can *find* a job in the city."

"So, do you want to work for me?"

Katie hesitated. "Aren't you afraid of what people will say?"

He sighed deeply. "Katie, I'm sorry about yesterday."

"I was expecting it from people like Mrs. Zook and her friends." She just hadn't expected it from him. It hurt, but she couldn't sustain the anger she wanted to feel. She knew he was simply protecting his family.

"I should have shown you the same support my mother did. Let me make up for my lapse of courage. Come work for me."

She needed work, but she hadn't planned on having to work beside Elam. She was already much fonder of him than was good for her. Whenever he was near, her heart charged into a gallop that left her feeling elated and breathless. Hopefully he didn't suspect. She would die of mortification if he realized how often her thoughts turned to him.

She glanced at his face as he waited for her reply. "I'll have to think on it. I've never done any weaving. I might not be any good at it."

"I can teach you what you need to know. You'll get the hang of it in no time. Come. I'll show you how it's done." He turned on his heels and strode toward the front of the barn. Surprised by his confidence in her ability to learn a new skill, Katie followed him.

He opened a door and stood aside for her to enter. Katie paused at the doorway. She rubbed her hands on her jeans. "This used to be the feed room."

"*Jah,* I turned it into my workroom because it had a good big window."

"Wasn't the window nailed shut?"

"I took the old one out and added more. Come in and see what else I have done. Here is where I keep the wood I use for the baskets. I like working with poplar. There's a big stand of them around the pond, so I don't have to buy the wood." His voice brimmed with eagerness to show her his work.

"I remember the poplars." She recalled

their shiny green leaves reflected in the calm waters of the pond in the summertime.

"I also use brown ash. These are some of my finished baskets." He gestured toward a bin beside the window.

Katie stepped inside the room. The aromatic scent of cedar and wood shavings enveloped her. Elam had painted the walls a bright white. Tools hung from pegs neatly arranged on one wall. A nearly completed cedar chest sat on a worktable. Its lid and a long hinge lay beside it waiting for him to assemble them. In the far corner of the room a tall cabinet stood open.

On the top shelf, Katie spied an Amish doll in a faded purple gown and black apron. It looked out of place among the tools and baskets.

She crossed the room and picked up the doll. Once she'd had one just like it. It had been a gift from her brother Hans. One of her few memories of him.

As she stared at the toy she noticed a small burn hole in the hem of the dress. Her doll's dress had had just such a hole. A burst of excitement sent her pulse racing. It couldn't be. Not after all these years. With shaky fingers she turned back the edge of the bonnet.

Thrilled, she spun around clutching the

doll to her chest. "You found Lucita."

The delight in her voice and the happiness shining in her eyes took Elam's breath away. He'd once wondered what it would take to make her smile at him. It seemed that he'd found the answer.

"Clearly, she must be one of your long-lost toys."

"It's my Lucita. Where did you find her?"

"She had been stuffed inside the wall through a gap in the boards. I found her when I was remodeling the place."

She was still hugging the toy. "My brother Hans gave her to me. It's the only thing I have from before the fire."

Elam stepped closer, happy that he had found the toy and kept it all these months. It was a simple Amish doll. The absence of facial features and hair was in keeping with the Amish obedience to the biblical commandment that forbade the creation of an image. It was dressed in typical Amish clothing, a deep purple gown that had faded over the years and a black apron and bonnet.

He said, "Lucita is an odd name for an Amish doll."

"Hans named her."

"Hans was the brother who died in the fire?"

She smiled sadly. "Yes. Hans saved my life that night. He carried me out wrapped in a blanket. I had Lucita in my arms. I suffered a few burns on my legs, but Hans was badly injured. Malachi told me he died a short time later."

"I'm sorry."

She shrugged. "It was a long time ago."

"How can you be sure it's your doll?"

She gave a guilty grin and pulled back the doll's bonnet to reveal a secret. "Hans used a marker to give her black hair like mine. I wanted someone who looked like me. All my family had blond hair. I always felt like I stuck out."

"Now you can give the toy to your daughter."

"I will, and I'll tell her it's a gift from her uncle Hans." Katie's smile was bright as the summer sun, and Elam basked in its warmth.

"You must tell her to take better care of Lucita than you did and not lose her."

Katie's smile faded. "Malachi took her away from me when I was seven. He said I was too old to play with dolls. He told me he threw her in the rubbish fire. Why would he hide her inside the wall?"

"I don't know. Perhaps he meant to give her back to you one day."

"I'd really like to believe that, but I don't think I can. He used to make me sleep out here when I did something that upset him. I think he enjoyed knowing he'd hidden the one thing that could give me comfort just out of sight."

"Why would your brother do something so cruel?"

"Because I caused the deaths of our whole family."

He stared at her in shock. "How could you? You were only a child."

"Malachi said I was the one who knocked over a kerosene lamp and set the house on fire. I don't remember doing it, but I remember seeing flames everywhere and screaming for help. Besides my mother, I lost Hans and two sisters, Emma and Jane. I can barely remember their faces. Malachi had recently married and had moved into this place. If he hadn't, he might have died, too."

Elam was deeply affected to hear how much she had suffered. He wanted to comfort her, but wasn't sure how. "Such things happen. It was a terrible tragedy, but it was God's will. It was not your fault. Your brother was wrong to blame you."

She straightened the bonnet on her doll's head. "I know. I tried so hard to earn his forgiveness when I was little. As I grew older, I resented his coldness and pretended I didn't care what he thought. The sad thing is . . . I really did care. I still do."

"Forgiveness is our way, Katie. Even if your brother cannot forgive you, you must forgive him."

"Easier said than done."

How could he ask it of her if he had not been able to do it himself? He sighed and smiled gently. "I know that well. But it does not change what is right."

Katie Lantz had brought turmoil into his orderly world, but she'd brought something else, too. She had a way of making him take a closer look at his own life, his own short-comings. He strongly suspected that by the time she left, he would be a better man for having known her.

She drew a deep breath and looked up. "You were going to show me how to weave a basket."

He allowed her to change the subject, but he would always remember the sadness in her voice. It touched a place deep inside him. A place that he'd kept closed off after the death of his father and Salome's excommunication. He wasn't the only one who had suffered a loss.

Katie moved about the room looking at the tools. She stopped at the stove. "What are these trays for?"

"For soaking the wooden strips so they can be bent easily."

"Tell me everything I need to know." She gestured toward the stacked poplar logs.

He focused on his work and pushed his need to comfort her to the back of his mind. "My baskets are unique. They're handmade from strips of wood. I buy the plywood for the base, but I do all the cutting here. After a log is trimmed and the bark stripped off, I pound the log with a mallet to loosen the growth rings."

"Will I be hammering logs?"

"No."

"I'm stronger than I look."

"I've seen baby barn swallows hanging out of their nests who look stronger than you."

She opened her mouth to reply, but seemed to think better of it. Instead, she turned back to the wood on the sawhorse. "What do you do next?"

"Then I peel off splints, or strips. The splints are then shaved to get rid of the fuzzy layer between the growth rings. They are rolled up in coils and stacked here. I cut them to size when I'm ready to start a basket."

Picking up a splint, she laid it on the workbench. "Now what?"

"This is one of the forms we use." He began setting the strips in place to form the ribs of the basket. Katie moved to stand close beside him. The top of her head barely reached his shoulder. She tucked her hair behind her ear and leaned over his work to inspect it.

Among his people women never cut their hair. Out of modesty and reverence, they wore it in a bun under a *kapp*. Katie's head was uncovered. She had cut her hair.

She was not Amish. He had to remember that. He had to harden his heart against the influence of this woman who chose to be an outsider.

Only the more he was near her, the more impossible that became. How was he going to work with her day after day?

CHAPTER TWELVE

Two days later, Katie found herself seated at the long table in Elam's workshop. The air, already filled with the smell of fresh-cut wood and simmering dyes, was being flooded with giggles. Mary, Ruby and Sally sat at the same table watching Katie's fledgling attempts to weave.

"I thought you were making a candy basket." Ruby picked up Katie's project to examine it.

"I am."

"Aren't you afraid the candy will fall though the gaps?" Ruby chuckled as she pushed her fingers through the loose slats and wiggled them at Katie.

Snatching her work away from Elam's oldest sister, Katie said, "Very funny. It's better than my last one."

Sally rose to Katie's defense. "I'm sure she'll improve in time."

"Before I run out of trees?" Elam came in

carrying an armload of freshly cut wooden splints.

Katie rolled her eyes. "Another comedian in the family."

After slipping the poplar pieces into a large vat of warm water, he came to stand at Katie's elbow. "You aren't doing so badly. You should have seen Ruby's first piece. In fact, I think *Mamm* still has it in the attic. Shall I go get it?"

Ruby wove another band between the upright stakes of her heart-shaped basket. "Go. You can spend all day looking through that dusty place. I don't care."

"Because she burned it." Mary's honesty was rewarded with an elbow to the ribs. She promptly swatted her sister with a long wand of reed. Ruby grabbed it. The ensuing tug-of-war ended when the reed broke in two.

"Oops." Ruby held out her broken half to Elam.

He sighed and grinned at Katie. "See what I've had to put up with all my life? It's no wonder this venture isn't making much money."

"But it keeps you close as a family," Sally said.

"*Jah.* It does that." Mary snatched the reed from her sister and tossed both pieces in the trash.

Elam moved to the stove. "The poplar should be ready."

The women all rose to select the plywood bases and molds for the unit they would be working on. Katie didn't bother to get up. Working with the woods instead of the more pliable reeds required some skill. Looking at her poor example, she knew she wasn't ready to tackle a complicated piece, but she was determined to learn.

She watched closely as Elam and Mary began to construct large hampers. Ruby and Sally both worked on picnic baskets. Their labors didn't stem the flow of chatter. More than once Katie found herself chuckling at the women's stories of family life.

"Just the other day, Thomas smeared mud all over Monroe so he could stick straw on him and make him look like a porcupine crawling across the floor." Ruby added a double band of scarlet color to the middle of her piece.

Mary smothered a laugh. "Now where did he get such an idea?"

Ruby shot a look at her brother. "It seems *Onkel* Elam told the boys a story about finding a porcupine in the woodpile."

"I didn't tell Thomas to make Monroe into one."

Pointing at him, Ruby said, "No, but you told me to drop an egg on *Dat*'s hat from the haymow. Do you remember that?"

"I remember scrubbing milk cans for a month because you hit Bishop Stulzman."

Ruby held up her hands. "How was I to know the bishop had come to talk to Papa? Besides, from the hayloft door I could only see the hat, not the man. I shouldn't have let you take the blame for that one."

"It *was* my idea. You just had better aim."

Mary began cutting the top of her basket ribs in preparation for setting the rim in place. "No wonder your boys are so ornery."

Sally began looping strands of rattan over her rim. "*Jah,* Jesse says they get their high jinks from their mother."

Ruby's eyebrows shot up. "Oh, he does, does he?"

Startled by her tone, Sally looked up to find her sister-in-law scowling at her. She opened her mouth, but closed it again.

A smile tugged at the corner of Elam's lips. "I didn't realize your husband was so smart, Ruby."

Ruby's jaw dropped. Mary snickered.

Katie, quietly turning and tucking the ribs of her basket, said, "He must be smart. He married Ruby."

Ruby's eyes lit up. "That's right." She

poked her brother's arm.

Elam's face reflected his surprise. "I did not know you could be so sassy, Katie."

Sitting back with satisfaction, Ruby grinned. "I like you, Katie Lantz. You're a quick wit."

"But not a quick basket weaver. I'm stumped. How do I attach the rim?" Katie was amazed at how easily she fit in with this family, and how accepting of her they were.

Sally moved her chair closer to Katie. "Use the thicker strips of flat, oval reed. One on the inside and one on the outside."

"I don't have enough hands to hold it all in place."

From her pocket, Ruby pulled a half-dozen wooden clothespins and slid them across the table. "Use these to clip the reed in place. They'll be your extra hands."

Sally demonstrated and Katie leaned in to watch as the younger woman used dyed sea grass to lash the rim pieces to the top row of the basket. When Sally was done, she handed it to Katie. "It's yours to sell now."

Katie looked at Elam. "Speaking of selling, how does that work?"

"Once a month, I take our products to a shop in Millersburg. The owner sells them for us. He takes orders at his shop and from mail catalogs and also from their Internet site, then he gives them to me to be filled."

"How many kinds of baskets do you make?" She looked at the variety in the bins.

"We have twenty different types, from laundry hampers to little trinket boxes." Mary stood and placed her hand in the small of her back as she stretched.

"Our best sellers are these picnic baskets. What do you think?" Ruby held up her finished container. It was the fanciest piece on the table, with double bands of scarlet color in the middle and a strip of scarlet rattan lashed around the top.

Katie tipped her head to the side. "It's very nice, but not plain."

Ruby smiled. "It's for the tourists."

Elam took it from his sister. "They come to see us Plain folk, but they like bright colors in their quilts and souvenirs. I'll put a lid and handles on this."

As Elam went to work with his small hand drill at the adjacent workbench, Katie couldn't help but admire the view of his broad shoulders, slim waist and trim hips. His homemade dark trousers and shirt accentuated his physique. She especially liked the way his hair curled in an unruly fashion, defying the typical "bowl style" haircut Amish men wore.

"He is a fine-looking man," Sally said quietly.

Katie, feeling the heat of a blush in her cheeks, glanced at Sally. Both Mary and Ruby were busy teasing each other and hadn't heard the remark. "He's well enough, I guess."

That produced a smothered giggle. "Far better than some I've met here. He will make a fine husband."

Katie tried to sound nonchalant. "Is there someone special?"

"Elam doesn't attend the singings on Sunday nights. Ruby and Mary fear he plans to remain single. They are hoping he'll be interested in Karen Imhoff, but I don't think he will be," Sally said.

"Why not?"

"She's *en alt maedel,* an old maid. She's twenty-five and never been married."

At twenty-two, Katie didn't consider twenty-five to be that old. Katie decided it was best to steer the subject away from Elam's single status. "Do you attend the singings?"

"*Jah.* I'll be seventeen next month. My mother says it's time I started looking for a husband."

"Don't be in a big hurry to give up your freedom."

185

Sally scooted her chair closer. "I'm not. I want to see and do things before I settle down. You've lived among the English. What was it like? Tell me about the music and dancing and movie stars."

Katie glanced at Elam's back. "I don't think I should."

"You're the only one I know who has lived away from this place."

It was hard to ignore the pleading in Sally's eyes. Katie, too, had dreamed about a world beyond the farm and the endless work. "I understand how you feel. Believe me, I do."

The door opened and Nettie came in, a bright smile on her face. "Rachel is awake and she wants her mama."

"I'm coming." Happy for any excuse to leave, Katie rose and left Sally's questions unanswered.

While she wouldn't mind satisfying Sally's curiosity, she knew Elam would object. The last thing she wanted was to upset the man who was giving shelter to her and her child.

"How goes life on the Sutter farm?"

Katie smiled at Amber as she began undressing Rachel for her one month examination.

"It's okay, I guess."

Elam had insisted on bringing her and the baby into Hope Springs for Rachel's visit with the doctor. Katie had enjoyed the ride seated beside him, but they had both remained silent. It seemed whenever they were together a kind of tension filled the air between them.

Amber glanced at Katie closely. "You don't sound like it's okay."

"You mustn't think I'm ungrateful. I can't begin to repay the Sutters for all they have done for me."

"So what's the problem?" Amber placed Rachel, naked and kicking, on the infant scale. The baby promptly voiced her disapproval with a piercing cry.

Katie leaned forward. "How much does she weigh?"

"Eight pounds nine ounces."

"That's good, right?"

"Very good. She's passed her birth weight. The doctor will be in in a few minutes." After measuring the baby, Amber swaddled her in a blanket and handed her back to her mother.

Katie shouldered the baby and patted her until she stopped fussing. "Amber, did you learn of any work in the area?"

Picking up a spray bottle of antiseptic, Amber misted the scale and then wiped it down with a paper towel. "I thought you were working for Elam Sutter and his mother?"

"I am, but I thought maybe I could find something else."

Amber regarded Katie closely. "Is Mr. Sutter working you too hard? Because if he is . . ."

Katie quickly shook her head and looked down. She couldn't stop the soft smile that curved her lips. "No, it's nothing like that. Elam has been very kind."

"Is Nettie chafing to have you out of the house?"

"Not that I can tell. She spoils the baby every chance she gets."

The puzzled expression on Amber's face changed to a look of understanding. "Oh. I see how it is. You poor thing."

Katie frowned at her. "What's that supposed to mean?"

"Elam's very kind, but you don't want to work for him. His mother adores your baby and spoils her, but you don't want to live with her. I'm getting the picture."

"I don't know what you're talking about."

"You know, it shows when you say his name."

Katie dropped her gaze. "You're talking nonsense."

"I don't think I am. Your eyes light up when you say Elam."

"They do not. You're being ridiculous."

"No, I'm not. Say his name."

"Stop it."

Amber propped her hands on her hips. "You can't do it without blushing."

"Because you're embarrassing me."

Pulling over a chair, Amber sat beside Katie. "I'm sorry to tease you. Are you thinking of joining the Amish church?"

"I've considered it, but I'm not sure. Sometimes I think it would make things easier."

"Don't do it if you're not certain that's where your heart lies."

"It's hard to know what to do. I wanted to get away from here so badly, yet now that I'm back things are different. No matter what I want, I have to think of what's best for Rachel. It isn't that I want material things for her. I want her to know she is loved and accepted. I want her to feel safe and secure."

"She can have those things in the Amish world or in the English one."

"I'm not sure that's true. I couldn't have given her any of that without Matt to help me in the city. Here, you've seen how Nettie dotes on Rachel. It's the same with everyone

189

in the Sutter family. Rachel will be taken care of in this community. She will belong."

"Joining a church for your daughter's sake isn't the same as doing it because you feel God has called you to that life. Do you feel called?"

It was a question Katie couldn't answer. Was she being called or was she just searching for something she'd never had?

The outer door opened. Katie looked up in relief as a white-haired man in a pale blue lab coat walked in. His smile was kindly and vaguely familiar. "Good afternoon. I'm Dr. Harold White. You must be Katie Lantz."

Katie shook the hand he held out. "It's nice to meet you, Dr. White."

He sat down on a metal stool and rolled it close. "I remember you now. You were only three or four at the time, so I shouldn't be surprised if you don't remember me. I treated your burns after your family's house fire. Terrible, sad business that was."

Katie still bore the scars on her legs. "I think I remember you. Did you know my family well?"

"Not really. Your mother hadn't been in the area very long. I do remember hearing that she had immigrated to the United States from Belize."

This was the first that Katie had heard of

such a thing. "My family came from Central America?"

"I believe so. I know several colonies of Old Order Amish exist in Belize."

Amber handed Dr. White Rachel's chart, then grinned at Katie. "That's the fun thing about working with Dr. White. You learn something new every day."

He chuckled. "A day I don't learn something new is a wasted day."

Katie smiled, but her mind was reeling. Why hadn't Malachi told her this? Was it possible she still had family in another country? She'd often wondered why she didn't have grandparents and cousins when everyone else at school had such big extended families. All Malachi ever said was that all her family was gone. If they had come from Central America, her doll's Spanish name made much more sense.

Dr. White placed his stethoscope in his ears and directed his attention to Rachel. "Let's have a listen to this little one."

After he had checked her over and pronounced her in excellent health, Katie asked, "Dr. White, is it possible to find out exactly where my family came from?"

He rubbed his chin. "I reckon the State Department would have to have some kind of records. Would you like me to check into it for you? I know a fella that used to work for them."

"I don't want to make extra trouble for you." Katie wasn't going to get her hopes up. Surely, if they had family anywhere Malachi would have mentioned it.

Dr. White chuckled. "I enjoy a challenge. It keeps me young. Besides, everything can be done on computers these days. Amber, have you drawn blood from Rachel?"

"Not yet, Doctor."

Katie frowned. "Why does she need blood drawn?"

Turning aside to make a note on the chart, Dr. White said, "It's just routine newborn screening."

"Shall I do the extended panel?" Amber asked.

He looked at Katie. "Is the baby's father of Amish or Mennonite descent?"

Katie shook her head. "No. What difference does that make?"

Gathering her supplies and pulling on a pair of latex gloves, Amber said, "Because the Amish and Mennonites are almost all descended from a relatively small group of ancestors, there are some inherited diseases that show up more frequently in their children."

Dr. White closed the chart and rose. "It's

unlikely that you'll have to worry about any of those. Just do the regular lab, Amber. I'd like to see Rachel again in three months and at six months."

"I may not be here then."

"Where will you be?" he asked.

"I'm not sure."

"Well, wherever you settle, she needs her well-baby checkups at least that often."

Katie had been focused on earning enough money to pay back the people who had helped them. She hadn't considered where she would go if she left Hope Springs.

Where did she want to settle?

Out in the waiting room, Elam put down the gardening magazine he'd been leafing through and glanced at the clock. What was taking so long? Rachel was a happy, healthy baby. Surely there wasn't anything wrong with her.

He had work to do. If he'd been thinking clearly, he would have let his mother bring Katie and the baby to town. The truth was, he hadn't been able to pass up this chance to spend time alone with Katie.

He had no idea how long she'd be staying with them. He had begun to cherish the minutes and hours he spent in her company, knowing it would end soon. It was foolish

— he knew that — but his heart could not be persuaded otherwise.

He heard a door open and glanced toward the hallway leading back to the exam rooms. Katie came out with Rachel in her arms. Amber walked beside her. The two women exchanged hugs and Katie turned to him. She was grinning from ear to ear.

He smiled back as his heart flipped over in his chest. No amount of rationalization or denial could change the fact that he was falling for this woman. And those feelings were growing every day.

Rising to his feet, he waited until she reached him. "You look happy about something."

"I've been learning so much about my family. My mother brought us here from Central America."

With her at his side, they left the doctor's office. He helped her into the buggy, using the excuse to hold her hand as she stepped up. "Your brother never mentioned this?"

"No, and I can't imagine why not. Dr. White is going to find out exactly where we came from and if any of my family still live there. I could have aunts, uncles and cousins I never knew about." Her eyes sparkled with exhilaration.

"I suppose it's possible." If she found she

had family in Central America, would she travel there? Sending her to Kansas would be hard enough, but he at least had some hope of seeing her again if she stayed with her brother.

She gripped her hands together. "It's so exciting."

He hated to burst her bubble, but he didn't want her getting her hopes up. "It's possible, but don't you think it's unlikely?"

As he feared, the excitement drained from her face. "I guess it is. I'm being silly, aren't I?"

"No. I don't think you're silly at all." He maneuvered Judy out into traffic.

She looked at him and said, "I am being silly. It's just —"

"Just what?" he prompted.

She blushed and looked down. He longed to lift her chin and see what was in her eyes, but Judy shied at a passing car and he turned his attention back to his driving.

Sitting up straighter, she asked, "When will you start planting your pumpkins?"

"In the next week or two."

The rest of the way home, they talked about everything from pumpkins to his mother's interest in Mr. Imhoff. It was a pleasant journey, but he got the feeling

Katie was deliberately steering him away from her conversation with Dr. White.

CHAPTER THIRTEEN

Over the next weeks, Elam found himself constantly making excuses to spend time with Katie and Rachel. Holding the baby and playing with her became his normal evening pastime. He was pleasantly surprised by Katie's aptitude and fast-growing skill at weaving. She had a good eye for color combinations and weaving patterns, and she had nimble hands. Some of her pieces were as good as Ruby's, and his sister had been weaving for over a year.

Late one evening, he was leaving the barn after tending to a sick colt when he passed the workroom and saw a light shining from under the door. He opened it to find Katie seated at the table with pen and paper in front of her, making a sketch. He almost left without disturbing her, but something drew him in.

"What has you up so late, Katie?"

Her gaze shot toward him. She laid both

197

hands over her drawing. "I couldn't sleep. I had an idea and I wanted to see if I could make it work."

"Let me see this idea." He entered the room, but she snatched the paper and held it behind her back before he could get a peek.

"It's nothing. You'll think it's silly."

"I've been making baskets for many years. If the idea has merit, I will know."

He approached the table and took a seat across from her. It was just the two of them. The lamp made a cozy circle of light. For an instant, it was almost possible to believe they were alone in the world. She was so beautiful it hurt his heart to look at her, but neither could he look away.

Nervous under his scrutiny, she licked her lips.

Ah, Katie. You have no idea how much I want to kiss you.

He forced his eyes away from her full red lips and held out his hand. "Let me see it. I may save you hours of frustration later."

Unfortunately, there would be no one to save him from the frustration of having her near and not being able to touch her. He'd been foolish to give her this job, to let her stay in his home. The price he would have to pay for such foolishness was becoming more apparent day by day. His heart was breaking by inches.

She smiled shyly and pushed the paper across the table. On it he saw a sketch of a bowl basket with a spiral weave curving around the sides like the stripes on a peppermint candy. "I saw one like this a long time ago and never forgot it. Is it possible to make one like this?"

As he studied it, he could see how a new mold would need to be made to shape the bowl just so. It might take some trial and error to find the right angle to form up the ribs. "What type of wood are you planning to use?"

"I don't know. What do you think?"

"Maybe a mix of light and dark maple. I could make a solid wood lid with a wooden knob on it for a top. It would be very fancy."

"Too fancy?" She reached to take the paper from him, but he held on to it.

"Not too fancy to sell."

It was definitely different from anything he'd seen in the gift shops. It was an eye-catching piece. "If they do well, I'll have to give you a larger commission."

"You really think it's *goot?*" The delight in her eyes shone as bright as the lamp.

He couldn't believe how happy it made him to see her smile. *"Jah,* Katie. It is very *goot.*"

She dipped her head. "*Danki,* Elam. More money is what I need."

His smile faded. Allowing Katie to earn more money meant that she would leave that much sooner.

It was the thing he wanted . . . and the thing he now dreaded.

Katie watched the play of emotions across Elam's face. What was he thinking? She knew the local gossips were linking his name with hers. His mother and his sisters tried to downplay the impact of the talk, but she wasn't fooled. They were beginning to worry. The family had suffered so much when their father was shunned. She didn't want to cause more pain.

He rose to his feet and picked up the lamp. "It is late. You should get some rest."

She stood and walked to the door with him. "Rachel will be awake soon. Once I've fed her I'll go back to bed and try to sleep."

"What troubles your sleep? Or is it that our beds are not as soft as the English like."

"The bed is fine. I just have a lot on my mind."

"Give your cares over to God."

Pulling her coat from a peg by the door, she slipped into it. "Good advice, but hard to follow."

As she walked out the door he nodded. It was true for him, as well.

At the house, they found Nettie reading her Bible in the living room. She held Rachel in the crook of one arm. Peering over the top of her glasses at them, she asked, "What have you two been up to?"

"Katie has been drawing up plans for a new basket design."

Blushing, Katie said, "I was just playing with an idea. Elam saw how to make it work."

"I'd like to see this plan. Elam, would you take this child. She's put my arm to sleep."

He lifted Rachel from his mother and carried her to the sofa where he sat down. "You are getting heavy. What are we going to do about that? Oh, I see. It's your eyelids that are getting heavy. Well, don't mind me. Go back to sleep."

Katie smiled at the pair. Elam was so good with Rachel. He was never impatient, always gentle. It was easy to see he cared a great deal for her daughter. He would make a good father someday.

He glanced up at her. As their eyes met, an arch of awareness passed between them. She knew by the look in his eyes that he felt it, too. How had this happened? When had she fallen in love with Elam?

On the last Saturday in April, Elam packed his baskets into the back of the buggy and prepared for the three-hour round trip into Millersburg. He wasn't surprised when Nettie announced that she and Katie would be joining him.

Attired in her newest dress and her Sunday bonnet and cape, Nettie climbed into the buggy. "What a nice spring day we have for our trip. I can't believe it's already the middle of April."

Elam found it hard to believe that Katie and Rachel had been with them for over a month. Katie had proven herself to be a hard worker and he knew she was making his mother's life easier by helping her with household chores. "I'll be able to get started with planting soon if the weather holds."

"And I need to get my garden in, but first we'll have a fine shopping trip. I want to go to the superstore and then I may need to stop at the fabric store. What are you needing, Elam?"

"Some new drill bits and blades for my wood plane. I also want to pick up some new dyes and coils of maple splints."

"Maple?" His mother looked at him in surprise. "I thought you only used poplar and ash in your baskets."

"We are trying something new with Katie's design. What about you, Katie? What are you needing in town?" Taking the baby from her, he helped her in and then handed up Rachel when Katie was settled.

"A few things for Rachel and a new pair of jeans. It shouldn't take me long to find what I need."

"*Goot,* then we will not have to spend much time in the city."

The buggy rocked in his direction when he stepped in, tipping Katie toward him. With Rachel in her arms, she couldn't catch herself. He threw up a hand to steady her. It landed at her waist. Her cheeks flamed crimson. When she regained her balance he withdrew his hand, but the feel of her slender torso remained imprinted in his mind.

Katie moved as far over as she was able, but it was still a tight fit with her sandwiched between him and his mother. It was going to be a long ride. He didn't know how he'd keep his attention on the road with her soft body pressed against his.

Each jolt in the road threw them against one another and sent waves of awareness tingling along his nerve endings. The sweet fragrance of her hair was like a tempting flower beside him. Judy tossed her head anxiously each time a car passed them, and he knew he was communicating his nervousness to the animal. Fortunately, they soon turned into the lane leading to Ruby's home.

Ruby had volunteered to keep Rachel so Katie would be free to enjoy her shopping trip. She came out of the house to meet them. "Sally is wanting to go with you, Elam. Do you mind one more?"

Sally came flying out of the house. "Please say I can go!"

Elam cast his gaze skyward. "What do you need in the city?"

"Some new shoes."

He frowned at her. "You can't find them in Hope Springs?"

"They'll be cheaper in Millersburg. I won't be any trouble. I promise."

"You'll have to squeeze in back with my cargo."

"That's fine. Thank you." She quickly climbed in the backseat, pushing aside several of the baskets.

Ruby moved to stand beside Elam. "Thanks for taking her. Can I have that fine baby girl now?"

Katie handed Rachel to him, a look of apprehension on her face. "I've never left her for so long."

Elam knew exactly how she felt as he handed the baby to his sister. "Don't let the boys turn her into a porcupine."

Gathering Rachel close, Ruby smiled at her. "Don't worry. I'll keep a good eye on her."

Katie handed out a bag with diapers and formula in it. "I know you will. Thanks again for watching her."

"My pleasure." Ruby waved as Elam turned Judy and drove out of the yard.

Back on the highway, the mare managed a brisk trot, but she was no match for the cars that went zinging past. It wasn't the local drivers he minded. They shared the road with only occasional complaints. It was the out-of-towners and teenagers he worried about. The ones who didn't know enough to slow down when they crested a hill, in case a buggy was just over the rise and out of sight. At fifty-five miles an hour, a car could run up on an Amish vehicle before the driver knew it. In such crashes, the car always won.

They had been on the road for an hour when a white van came flying past and honked loudly. The noise spooked the horse, but Elam was able to keep her under control. His temper was harder to hold in check. "Foolish English. They're looking to get someone killed."

"Calm yourself, Elam," his mother said.

She was right. What good did it do to show his temper to his family?

The next car that passed them slowed when it drew alongside. As soon as he saw the camera aimed his way, he pulled off his hat to shield his face. The Plain People felt photographs were graven images and forbidden by the Bible. His mother turned away, as well. To his surprise, so did Katie. As the car sped on, he looked at Katie with a new respect. It was good to see she still practiced some of the Amish ways.

After another half hour of travel, Sally, sitting behind him, leaned forward. "Does anyone know some new jokes?"

For the next mile they exchanged funny stories and jokes that had all the women laughing. Elam put up with it.

Finally, Katie prodded Elam with her elbow. "Knock, knock."

"This is silliness," he stated firmly.

" 'A merry heart doeth good like a medicine: but a broken spirit drieth the bones,' " his mother quoted from *Proverbs.*

Katie repeated, "Knock, knock."

He rolled his eyes heavenward. "Who's there?"

"Amish."

He glared at her from the corner of his eye. "Amish who?"

She playfully draped her arm around his shoulders. "Ah, I miss you, too."

Katie regretted her impulsive hug the moment she felt Elam stiffen. Self-consciously, she withdrew her arms and folded her hands in her lap. Nettie and Sally were laughing, but he wasn't. Had she made him angry with her forward behavior?

"That's a good one," Nettie declared.

"A bunch of silliness," Elam stated again, but as Katie glanced his way she saw the corner of his mouth twitching.

She said, "The English don't think the Amish have a sense of humor."

"Oh, but we do," Nettie declared, still chuckling.

"Have you heard the one about the Amish farmer with twin mules?" Elam asked.

"No." Katie relaxed and listened to his joke with a light heart. It felt good to be included and accepted by Elam and his family. The trip into town became a happy jaunt as they all tried to outdo each other with funny stories. Katie was sorry when the outskirts of Millersburg came into view.

The first stop was a busy gift shop where Elam carried in his baskets. Katie followed, eager to see how her weaving design would be greeted. Of course, it had been Elam who perfected the pieces, but she had had a hand in their creation. The owner showed enough interest to order a dozen more bowls and to add a photo of one to his online catalog.

With the cargo disposed of, Katie joined Sally in the backseat. Sally, eager to see as much of the small city as possible, rolled up the rear flap and was almost hanging out. "Did you see the dresses in that store window?"

"I saw them." Katie was sure the prices were well above what she could afford.

Sally checked to make sure Nettie and Elam weren't listening. In a low voice she said, "My friend Faith has clothes like that. She sneaks out of the house and goes out on dates with English boys. They go to movies and smoke cigarettes. Faith says she's going to make the most of her *rumspringa*."

It was a common enough occurrence in Amish communities. Teenagers often rebelled against their strict upbringing. Most families in Katie's more liberal district tolerated such behavior and waited for it to end. When the teenagers reached marrying age, most settled down, made their baptisms and led quiet lives. Most, but not all.

"Is that what you want to do?" Katie asked.

Sally averted her gaze. "I don't know. It sounds like fun, but my folks would be so disappointed and ashamed if I was caught doing something like that."

"Only if you were caught?"

Sally's eyes snapped to meet Katie's. She didn't reply, but her mood became pensive. After a while, she said, "I noticed you weren't at the last church service. Will you be going tomorrow?"

"I'm not sure." Katie had been considering it but she didn't know if she was ready to face Bishop Zook again. He was sure to ask if she was ready to start instructions for baptism.

At the superstore, Elam secured Judy to one of the dozen hitching rails in a special section of the parking lot, and the group headed through the large sliding glass doors. By unspoken consent, the women became reserved and quiet. When they were out in the English world, they did nothing to attract attention to themselves.

Inside, Elam turned to his mother. "I will not be long. I know where the tools are. Where shall we meet?"

Sally turned around slowly, awe written on her face.

Nettie pulled a red shopping cart from the line. "I may be a while. I need several bolts of fabric and some thread. Hopefully they will have the sewing machine needles I need here and we won't have to go to another store."

Spinning to face her, Sally said, "I don't mind if we have to visit more stores."

"I'm sure it won't take me long to find things for Rachel. Why don't we meet in the food court," Katie suggested, gesturing to a collection of booths and fast-food counters off to the side of the doorway.

Elam smiled and rubbed his stomach. "*Jah,* a cheeseburger and French fries sounds yummy."

Katie grinned. Eating out was a rare treat. One enjoyed by every member of the family.

Nettie took Sally's hand. "Let's see if we can find you some shoes that fit. Then you can help me pick the fabric for my new dresses."

Elam strode toward the hardware department as Nettie and Sally went in the other direction. Left alone, Katie strolled through the store. Row after row of bright summer clothes in every color of the rainbow beckoned her. After trying on several pairs of jeans and finding one that fit, Katie draped them over her arm and left the dressing room.

A pair of teenage girls were holding up tank tops and shorts in front of a mirror. Katie stopped beside them to hang up a pair of pants she didn't want. As she did, one of the girls began snickering and pointing. Katie followed their gaze to see what was so funny. She saw Sally admiring the shimmering material of a dress on one of the mannequins.

What a contrast. Sally wore a simple dark blue dress beneath her black cape. Black stockings and sturdy black shoes with little heels adorned her feet. Her head was covered with a wide-rimmed bonnet. They were the same style of clothes every Amish woman wore. Yet so much more than clothes separated Sally from these other young women.

Katie's thoughts turned to Rachel. Which world did she want for her daughter? Until Katie had met Elam and his family, her choice seemed simple. Now she was seeing the Amish in a new light. Her brother's views weren't the views of all Plain people. Malachi was an unhappy man who took his sour mood out on those around him. She understood that now.

One of the shopping teens pulled out her

cell phone and snapped a picture of Sally. "Why do they dress so stupid?"

Katie answered the girl, although she knew the question hadn't been directed at her. "They dress that way because they wish to be separate from the world. Their clothing and even the shape of their head coverings identify them as part of a special group."

"What does being separate from the world mean?" the other girl asked.

"That they have chosen to live a life they believe is pleasing to God. To do that, they must reject worldly things such as electricity and cars, bright colors and jewelry, even phones."

"No electricity, no TV, no iPods — that's just dumb." The taller girl shook her head and the two of them laughed as they resumed their shopping.

Katie threaded her way between racks of clothes on her way to the infant department. How funny was it that she should be the one explaining about Amish practices? Matt would be laughing his head off if he were still around.

With a start, she realized she hadn't thought about Matt in days. The man occupying her thoughts lately had been Elam. She thought about his ready smile, the way he was always willing to help his mother or his sisters with their work in addition to his own. The way he enjoyed talking to and rocking Rachel in the evenings. He was so different from her brother. So different from Matt.

Katie had to admit she was falling hard for Elam. Her head told her there was no future there, but the heart rarely paid attention to what was smart.

As Katie rounded the corner into the infant section, she stopped short at the sight of a beautiful baby dress on display. Pink satin with short, puff sleeves trimmed with lace, it had a row of pearl buttons and bows down the front. Katie reached out to finger the silky cloth.

"Is that how you want Rachel to grow up?"

She turned to see Elam leaning on a shopping cart behind her.

He nodded toward the dress. "Do you want her to value fancy clothes, to think our ways are stupid?"

"Of course I don't."

But once she had felt that way. Until a few weeks ago Katie had been determined to return to the outside world. She had a choice now.

Elam straightened and stepped closer. "I heard what you said to those young women.

You said we have chosen to live a life that is pleasing to God."

"That's what I was taught."

"But is it what you believe?"

Was it? It was hard to put into words what she believed. No one had ever asked her that question. Elam stood quietly waiting for her answer. She said, "I believe people of all faiths can choose to live a life that is pleasing to God."

His eyes bored into hers. "Is that what you are doing, Katie? Are you living a life that pleases God?"

CHAPTER FOURTEEN

Katie had no answer for Elam's questions. Instead, she said, "It won't take me long to get what I need for Rachel, then I'll be ready to leave."

"All right. I'll wait for you in the food court." As he turned away, she glimpsed a deep sadness in his eyes and couldn't help wondering why he cared so much.

When she had what she needed, she crossed the store to the sewing center. She found Nettie talking to another Amish woman next to a table of solid broadcloth bolts in an array of colors. Lavenders, purples, darker greens, mauves and even pinks were all acceptable colors for dresses in their church district.

Nettie caught sight of Katie and nodded in her direction. The other woman glanced her way, said something else to Nettie and then walked off without acknowledging Katie.

Nettie held up a length of green fabric. "What do you think of this one?"

"I like the mauve better."

"For me, yes, but for you this dark green would be a good color."

"You don't need to make me a dress."

"No, but I want to. I'm tired of seeing you in those jeans all the time. Now don't argue with me."

Katie debated a moment, then said, "All right."

Nettie's brows shot up in surprise. "You aren't going to argue?"

"If you want to make me a dress, I won't stop you."

A slow smile spread across Nettie's features. "And you will wear it to church services tomorrow?"

So that was the hitch. Katie's conversation with the young shoppers and with Elam came to mind. Perhaps it was time she started living a better life and not just existing in her present one.

Anyway, just because I go to a church service doesn't mean I'm thinking of joining the Amish faith. Does it?

Was she really considering returning to the strict, devout life she once hated? To her surprise, she found that she was.

She met Nettie's hopeful gaze and nodded. "*Jah.* I will wear the dress to tomorrow's preaching."

"*Wundervoll.* I was worried you would refuse." Nettie's relief was so evident that Katie instantly became suspicious.

"Who was the woman you were talking to when I came up?"

Nettie busied herself with choosing thread to match her fabric. "Oh, that was the new deacon's wife."

"What did she want?"

"Eada was shopping for fabric, the same as me."

"But she said something that upset you. I saw your face."

"Eada likes to repeat gossip, that's all."

"And the gossip was about me." A horrible sensation settled in the pit of Katie's stomach.

"It's nothing. Nothing. Where did I put my purse?"

"Nettie, you don't lie well."

Sighing in resignation, Nettie said, "Some of the elders don't like that you are staying under the roof of an unmarried man. I said, 'What am I? A doorpost?' I chaperone you."

"Oh, Nettie, the last thing I want is to make trouble for you and Elam."

"Talk will die down when they see what a fine woman you have become."

Katie wasn't so sure. Her old insecurities raised their ugly heads. She'd never fit in before. What made her think she could fit in now?

The following morning Katie was the last one to leave the house. Nettie was already waiting in the buggy. Elam stood at the horse's head.

Katie slanted a glance in his direction. He gave her a gentle smile. "You look Plain, Katie Lantz."

From Elam, it was a wonderful compliment. She knew she had to be blushing.

The dark green dress and white apron she had on fit her well enough. Made without buttons or zippers, the dress required pins to fit it to the wearer. To Katie, it felt strangely comforting to be back in Plain clothes. It was the only thing comforting about the morning. Worrying about how she would be accepted at the service had her stomach in knots.

Katie handed Rachel up to Nettie. The baby, swaddled in a soft, white woolen blanket, wore a small white bonnet. Katie had borrowed a *kapp* from Nettie for herself, but wisps of her short hair kept escaping her hairpins. She might pass for an Amish woman to an outsider, but the

218

church members would know differently.

The trip to services took nearly half an hour. With each passing mile Katie became more nervous. When the farm came into view, she drew a deep, ragged breath and tried to brace her failing courage.

Suddenly, she felt Elam's hand on hers. He didn't say anything, but the comfort in his simple touch gave her the strength she need. After a long moment, he let go to guide the horse into the yard. When he pulled the horse to a stop, Katie was ready.

She took her place beside Nettie and her daughters on one side of the room. After the first hymn the preaching started. As she listened to the minister, she noticed two little girls in front of her squirming on hard benches. Some things never changed.

At one point, Katie left to nurse her baby. In one of the bedrooms at the back of the house, a second young mother on the same mission joined her.

Katie learned the woman was Bishop Zook's daughter-in-law, the wife of Aaron Zook and a neighbor of Elam's. As the two of them exchanged pleasantries, Katie learned their children were almost the same age. Discussing their infant's temperaments, their funny quirks and motherly concerns made Katie see she wasn't that different from any mother, Amish or otherwise.

When Rachel was satisfied, Katie returned to her place beside Nettie. The second sermon, conducted by Bishop Zook, was heartfelt and moving.

A great sense of peace came over Katie. She held tight to the presence of Christ in her heart for the first time in a long, long time. All that she had worried about drifted away. She was one of God's children and she had been called to this place by His will.

Throughout the long service, Elam was constantly aware of Katie across the room from him. What was she thinking? Was she only pretending piety to stem the gossip or to appease his mother? He didn't want to believe it, but how could he be sure?

In spite of his best intentions, he had grown fond of Katie and Rachel. In his mind, it was easy to see them all becoming a family. What would it be like to spend a lifetime with Katie at his side? To see her bear his children? How he wanted to watch Rachel grow into a young woman, to see her marry and have children of her own.

These were things he wanted, but he kept them closed off inside his heart. He didn't dare give voice to them for if Katie took Rachel and left their community, he would grieve their loss more deeply than any other in his life.

When church came to an end, he followed the other men outside. It was warm enough that the homeowners had decided to set out the meal picnic style in the yard.

A volleyball net was soon up in place between two trees on the lawn. Several dozen of the younger boys and girls quickly began a game. The cheering and laughter from participants and onlookers filled the spring afternoon with joyous sounds.

Elam spied Katie watching the game, a wistful look on her face. She stood on the edge of the lawn by herself, except for Rachel in her arms.

Elam loaded two plates with fried chicken, coleslaw, pickled red beets, fresh rolls and two slices of gooey shoofly pie. He carried them to where she stood. "I've brought you something to eat."

She smiled and rolled her eyes. "What is this *thing* you have about feeding me?"

"I don't like skinny women." He held out one plate.

Lowering herself to the ground, she leaned back against the trunk of the tree and placed Rachel on her outstretched thighs.

"If you think I'm going to get fat just to make you happy, think again."

"One plate of food will not make you fat."

"Ha! Do you know how many calories are in that peanut butter and marshmallow spread?"

He sat beside her. "No, and I don't want to know."

She took the plate from his hand, set it on the grass and picked up the slice of home-made bread covered with the gooey spread. She bit into it and moaned. "Oh, this is good."

The words were no sooner out of her mouth than the volleyball came flying toward them. Elam threw out his hand to protect Rachel as the ball landed beside her. Katie caught it on the bounce. Holding her chicken between her teeth, she threw the ball back to the players.

Elam sat back, relieved they were both okay.

"Nice toss," Sally said as she dropped down at Katie's feet.

"It was a fluke. I don't have an athletic bone in my body."

"You didn't play ball when you were younger?" Elam asked.

"No." Shaking her head, Katie took another bite of her meal.

Sally scowled. "Why not?"

"Malachi didn't like it."

"Your brother sounds . . . *premlijch*."

Katie laughed. "Yes, *grumpy* is a good word for him."

Sally shot to her feet and grabbed Katie's arm. "Well, he's not here, so come and play."

"I can't. I have a baby to watch."

Laying his plate aside, Elam held out his arms. "I'll watch her."

"There! Now you have no excuse." Sally clapped her hands together.

After a moment of hesitation, Katie gathered Rachel close and turned toward Elam, a look of uncertainty in her eyes. "Are you sure you don't mind?"

In that moment, he knew Katie had wormed her way past all the defenses he'd set around his heart. He smiled and said, "Go."

Grinning, she handed him the baby and shot to her feet. Elam leaned back against the tree with Rachel propped against his shoulder as Katie joined the game in progress.

She missed the first ball that came her way. Hiding her face behind her hands, she doubled over laughing at her own foolishness. The second time the white ball came flying toward her, she hit a creditable return.

Hearing cheering for her, he twisted his head to see his mother and sisters sitting on

223

a bench near the house. Nettie and Ruby, their hands cupped around their mouths, were yelling instructions.

It seemed that Katie had wormed her way into more hearts than just his.

He glanced down at Rachel's sleeping face. "What have I let myself in for, little one?"

There was no help for it now. He was well and truly on his way to falling in love with Katie Lantz.

Katie felt like a kid again. No, she felt like the kid she'd never been allowed to be.

Racing over the fresh new grass, she chased a ball that she'd hit out of bounds. It rolled to a stop at the feet of Bishop Zook.

He said, "You are out of practice, Katie."

Breathless, she scooped up the ball and nodded to him. "*Jah,* I am."

"When your game is over, come and speak with me for a little while."

She felt her smile slip away. "Should I come now?"

Shaking his head, he said, "No, it will wait. Go and enjoy this beautiful day that God has made."

Katie returned to the game, but some of her enjoyment was lost. At the end of the match, she checked to see that Elam was still okay holding Rachel, then she excused herself and went to seek the bishop. She found him loading a large picnic basket into the back of his buggy.

"Are you leaving?" Maybe she could put off this conversation.

"In a little while. My wife and I are taking some food to Emma Wadler. Her mother is recovering from a broken hip and Emma is having a tough time running the inn and taking care of her."

"I think I remember Mrs. Wadler." It was easier to make small talk than to find out why the bishop wanted to see her.

"It was good to see you back among us, Katie, dressed Plain and attending services. It makes my heart glad. For we know there is more rejoicing in Heaven over one sinner who repents than over ninety-nine righteous ones who do not need to repent."

She looked down, unable to meet his gaze. "Thank you, Bishop."

"Many of us have doubts about the path God wishes us to follow."

Looking up, she asked, "Even you?"

"You have no idea how I struggled with my decision to become baptized."

"Really?"

He smiled at her. "Really."

"But you're a bishop."

"It was a path I never wished to trod, but *Gott* chose me. Without His help, I could do none of this. Let *Gott* be your help, Katie. Be still. Be at peace and listen with your heart to His council."

"I'm trying to do that."

"If you find *Gott* wishes for you to stay among us, we shall welcome you with open arms." He began rolling down the rear flap on his buggy.

Katie glanced to where Elam sat talking to Aaron Zook and his wife. Both men held the babies while the women of the congregation were busy packing up their hampers of leftover food. Numerous children, reluctant to give up their games, were kicking the ball across the grass with shouts of glee.

Wasn't this what she wanted? Didn't she long to be a part of a family, a part of a community? It wouldn't be an easy life, but it would be a life of belonging.

Impulsively, she turned back to the bishop. "When does *die Gemee nooch geh* begin?"

He paused in the act of fastening the leather flaps. "The class of instruction to the faith will be starting after the next church day."

"Thank you, Bishop."

He looked over her head. "Ah, here is my

wife. I believe there is something she wishes to say to you."

CHAPTER FIFTEEN

Elam unharnessed his draft horses on Monday evening and led them to the corral beside the barn. Turning them loose, he watched as they each picked a spot and began to turn around with their nose at ground level. Finally, they dropped to their knees, then rolled their massive bodies in the dirt. Wiggling like puppies, they thrashed about to scratch their backs and shake off the sweat of their long day in the fields.

Elam spared a moment to envy them. Planting was hard work, and he still had things in the woodshop waiting for him. After hanging and cleaning his harnesses, he strode to the front of the barn and opened the workroom door. Katie was seated at the table with a small heart-shaped basket in front of her.

He saw she had finished several already. "You are getting faster?"

"But am I getting better?" She held up

228

one for inspection.

He examined it closely "*Jah,* you are getting better."

Handing it back, he moved to his workstation and selected the tools he needed. A nearly finished rocking chair was waiting for him to carve a design into the headrest. He glanced over his shoulder. The frown of concentration on Katie's face made him smile.

Was she happy here? He wanted to ask, but he was afraid of the answer. Although she rarely talked about leaving any more, he'd never heard her mention another plan.

Would she stay if he asked her to? He looked back to the wood in front of him. He was afraid to ask. Afraid she might say no, and equally afraid she might say yes for all the wrong reasons. Instead, he said, "I thought Bishop Zook did a good job of preaching yesterday."

"He did. It was long and the benches haven't gotten any softer since I left, but I did find it comforting."

"I saw Mrs. Zook talking to you. Was she rude again?"

"No. She apologized for her earlier behavior."

He picked up his chisel. "Did she?"

"I can tell you I was stunned."

He chuckled. "You and me both."

"She said she'd let hearsay form her opinions and that she was aware that people could change."

"I reckon they can. What did you think of the service?"

"I enjoyed it."

"Enough to attend again?"

"I'm thinking about it."

He spun around to look at her. "You are?"

"*Jah.* I can tell you're stunned."

Moving to stand beside her, he said, "Maybe a little stunned but mostly happy."

They stood staring at each other for a long time. He wanted so badly to kiss her. He sucked in a quick breath and moved back to his workbench.

"Elam, can I ask you a personal question?"

"*Jah.*"

"What was she like, the girl you were betrothed to?"

He leaned forward and pushed his gouge into the wood, wondering how to answer that. "She was quiet. A hard worker."

"Was she pretty?"

"Yes." He kept his eyes on his task.

"How did you meet?"

"We grew up together. How did you meet Matt?"

"Matt and I met at the drugstore in Hope Springs. He was visiting some friends in the area. They were sitting at a booth and making fun of a young Amish boy who had come in."

"Is that what you liked about him? That he poked fun at us?"

"No. I felt sorry for the boy and I told Matt and his friends to stop it. I know I shouldn't have. We are to turn the other cheek."

"Rude behavior doesn't have to be tolerated."

"Anyway, after I left, Matt followed me and apologized. I thought it was very fine of him."

Her voice took on a soft quality. "He could be like that. One moment a good man, the next moment a spoiled child. I don't know what it was about him that blinded me to his true self."

"It is our own feelings that blind us."

"Were you blind to Salome's feelings?"

"*Jah.* When I finished school, my parents sent me to my uncle Isaac in Ontario to learn the woodworking trade. During those years I wrote to Salome every week. I told her about my plans for our life together."

"And she wrote back?"

"She did, but her letters were filled with

the day-to-day things. I should have known then that something was wrong, but I wasn't looking for the signs." It was the first time in a long time that he was willing to examine his feelings about those days.

"I know what you mean. Matt seemed so interested in me. The more I resisted his advances, the more interested he became. I was so flattered. I snuck out of the house to see him. Malachi caught us together one night. He was furious. He grabbed my arm and ordered Matt to leave. That's one thing about Matt — he hates to have anyone tell him what to do."

"And so it is with you, too."

"Perhaps that's true. To be honest, I jumped at the chance to defy Malachi."

"So you left with Matt."

"I did. I was honestly determined to make our relationship work, but he wasn't. He soon grew tired of being saddled with a stupid Amish girlfriend who couldn't drive a car or work the DVD recorder."

He turned around and came to sit beside her. Taking her hand, he said, "You aren't stupid."

She stared into his eyes for a long time. She had such beautiful dark eyes. He could almost see his future in them. Finally, she looked down. "It took me a while to start believing that. What happened between you and Salome?"

"It isn't important anymore." He started to rise, but she laid a hand on his arm and stopped him.

"It is important. Past wrongs have the power to hurt us if we don't let go of them."

The warmth of her small, soft hand on his skin sent a wave of awareness coursing through his body. He focused on her concerned face. "What makes you think I haven't let go?"

She tipped her head to the side. "Have you?"

"Perhaps not."

He longed to reach out and touch her face. How would she react? Would she pull away?

Such thoughts were folly. He should go. He had work to do. But he didn't rise. He sat there looking into her eyes and he saw himself as he had been when he was young and impressionable and sure of his place in the world. He wanted to share that part of his life with Katie.

"I returned home from my uncle's at the age of twenty-one, ready to settle down, start my own business . . . and marry. That spring I was baptized and took my vows to the church. Salome did the same. If only she had waited until she was certain of what she wanted."

"Don't judge her too harshly."

"I've begun to forgive her." As he said it, he realized it was true. She had hurt him, but how much more would they both have suffered if she had gone ahead with the wedding?

Glancing sideways at Katie seated beside him, he said, "When the date for our marriage approached she finally admitted the truth. She had used our engagement to keep her parents from pressuring her into marrying anyone else. She didn't love me."

"I'm so sorry."

"I thought maybe she saw some flaw in me."

"I don't see how. You're a good man, Elam."

She thought he was a good man. Well, he wasn't, Elam reflected bitterly. He struggled every day to live a life pleasing to God. Perhaps she understood that better than anyone, for she openly admitted her own struggles.

Katie said, "Why did she leave the church?"

"All the time I had been working for my uncle, Salome had been working for an English family as a nanny. I believe she tried to give up her life among the English, but she couldn't do it. Not when her employer offered to help her further her education. She told me she longed to go back to school, to learn things beyond what she needed to know to keep house and rear children."

Salome had turned her back on her family, on Elam and on his hopes and dreams. "My family, her family, we all tried to reason with her, but after several months it was clear that she wasn't going to return to the church. She was shunned, not because we didn't love her anymore, but in the hopes of making her reconsider her choices."

"Your mother told me your father also left the faith."

Elam bowed his head. "He did. I had to shun my own father. My mother couldn't bear it and asked to be excommunicated, too, so that they could live together as man and wife. It was a dark time."

Katie's heart went out to Elam. She squeezed his hand. "I'm so sorry. Was that why you moved to Ohio?"

"After *Dat* passed away, my mother came back to the church, but it was not the same for us. I saw an ad in the paper for farms for sale in Ohio. My brothers-in-law and I came to look the places over. Your brother was eager to sell to me. I got the land for a good price. We were blessed that Mary and Ruby found homes here, as well."

Katie hesitated before voicing the question she couldn't ignore. Finally, she asked gently, "Elam, was your mother wrong to leave the church to stay with your father?"

The sadness in his eyes was replaced by anger. "My father was wrong to leave the church."

"Your mother must have loved him very much."

"*Jah,* she loved him, but did he love her? I'm not so sure. What kind of love is it to make another suffer for your own doubts?"

He shot to his feet and left. Katie didn't try to stop him. She was happy that he'd been able to share this much about himself. All she wanted was to be near him and to make him happy.

She loved him, but loving a person was not enough. They had both learned that the hard way. He wasn't indifferent to her. She was woman enough to read the signs in his eyes, but he never spoke of it. She knew why.

Even if she found the courage to tell him of her love, she knew he'd never consider marriage to someone outside his faith. If she became Amish would it change how he felt about her? Or was she breaking her own heart by staying here?

The following afternoon, Katie was working in the woodshop when Elam poked his head in the door. She laid the basket aside, loving the way her heart skipped a beat each time he was near.

He said, "Katie, you have a visitor. Dr. White is here."

She frowned. "Dr. White? Why has he come to see me?"

Elam stepped closer, a look of concern on his face. "I don't know. Is Rachel okay?"

Katie rose to her feet. "He did take a blood test from her."

Had the results been serious enough to bring him out to the farm? She was aware that some Amish children suffered from inherited birth defects, but she hadn't seen any signs that Rachel was sick.

Please, God, don't let there be anything wrong with my baby.

Katie darted past Elam and hurried toward the house. Inside, Nettie had the good doctor settled at the kitchen table with a cup of coffee and a slice of her homemade cherry pie in front of him. He already had a forkful in his mouth.

Katie halted inside the door, striving to

keep calm. Elam came in and stood behind her. To her surprise, she felt his hands on her shoulders offering comfort and support.

She said, "Dr. White, what brings you out here?"

He finished chewing, then tapped his plate with his silverware. "If I had known that there was pie this good here, I've have come much sooner."

Nettie beamed. "I'm glad it's to your liking."

"If your family ever has need of medical care, you may pay the bill with pies, Mrs. Sutter."

Katie took a step forward. "Is there something wrong with Rachel's tests?"

The doctor shook his head. "No, everything is fine. After your visit, I got to thinking about your family and I did a little investigating with the help of my old college roommate. He's retired from the State Department, but he still has connections there. It turns out your family immigrated from a place called Blue Creek in Belize. Unfortunately, that's all my friend could find out. There isn't anyone left in the area with the name of Lantz or Eicher, which was your mother's maiden name. I'm sorry. I know you were hoping for a different answer."

Katie struggled to hide her disappointment and hold back tears. She knew the chances of finding more of her family had been remote, but she couldn't help getting her hopes up.

After the doctor thanked Nettie for her hospitality, he donned his hat and headed outside to his car. He opened the car door, then stopped. "I almost forgot. Nettie's pie drove it right out of my mind. Amber said to tell you she found a job you might like."

"She has? Where?"

"At the Wadler Inn. Now, it's only a temporary position, but it could turn into more. Emma Wadler is needing help because her mother has broken her hip, and Amber thought of you."

"I'll go and see her today."

As the doctor drove away, Katie heard the screen door slam. She looked toward the house to see Elam approaching. When he was close enough, he said, "I'm sorry, Katie. I know how much finding more of your family meant to you."

She turned and began walking toward the bench beneath the apple tree at the back of the yard. "It's just that I've wanted to be a part of a real family for as long as I can remember. I wanted to be a part of a family like yours. A place where people laugh and talk about their worries and their hopes. Where they get together on Sundays and travel to visit each other in their homes. I took that away from Malachi. I have to accept that he is my only family."

Elam grasped her arm and turned her to face him. "Katie, you can't keep blaming yourself."

"Oh, I know. I used to think I didn't deserve a family after what I'd done. I just needed to know there was someone out there who wanted me."

He opened his arms and she went to him. "Katie, you are already a part of a family. You are one of God's children. That makes you a part of His family. Wherever you go, no one can take that from you."

Wherever I go. He doesn't believe I will stay here.

She laid her cheek against his chest, drawing strength from him and comfort from his embrace. "You are a good man, Elam."

"And you're a good woman, Katie."

Giving a tiny shake of her head, she said, "A lot of people will disagree with that."

From the porch, his mother called his name. He slowly drew away from Katie. She missed his warmth like a physical ache. He gazed at her intently. "I stand by what I said."

She watched him walk to the house. She had been searching for a place to belong somewhere in the world, but what she really wanted was to belong here.

Was it possible? Elam's embrace had just given her a bright ray of hope.

CHAPTER SIXTEEN

"What is that long face for?" Nettie demanded as she sprinkled a packet of flower seeds into the freshly turned earth bordering the walkway.

On her knees clearing away last year's old growth, Katie sighed. How was she going to break the news to her friend? Pulling out a few early weeds, Katie said, "What if I told you I was moping because . . . I'm moving out."

"What is this? Where are you going?" Nettie propped her fists on her hips.

"I have a job at the Wadler Inn starting the day after tomorrow. Emma Wadler also owns a small apartment that I can rent starting in two weeks."

Turning away, Nettie wiped at her eye with her forearm. "I'm happy for you, but I will miss you."

"I'll come to visit often and you will see me at church. I've already talked to Bishop

Zook about taking instructions."

Nettie turned back, a wide smile on her face. "That's wonderful news."

"I thought you'd be happy to hear that."

"Have you told Elam?"

"Not yet." Katie looked down. She wasn't sure how Elam would take the news. Would he think she was only doing it because of her feelings for him?

There had been no repeat of the closeness they'd shared the day the doctor came to see her. She was half-afraid her growing love was making her see things that weren't there. Did Elam care for her the way a man cared for a woman, or was she reading what she wanted to see into his simple kindness?

Nettie brought up a hand to shade her eyes. "It looks like Elam is home from town."

Sitting back on her heels, Katie dusted off her hands and tried to calm her rapidly beating heart. She was surprised when he stopped the buggy in front of the house instead of driving it to the barn.

Stepping down, Elam came toward her, a pensive expression on his face. She stood, a sense of unease tickling the back of her neck. He held out a thick white envelope. "This came for you in the mail today."

"For me?" She took a step closer.

"It's from your brother."

Stunned, she took the letter from him and stared at the return address. Why had Malachi written? What did he want?

"Aren't you going to open it?" Elam prompted.

"Yes." She turned away and walked across the new green grass to the bench beneath the blooming apple tree. The pink flowers of the tree scented the air with their heady perfume. The drone of bees inspecting each open bud mingled with the soft sighing of the breeze in the branches.

Sitting down, she opened the envelope with trembling hands and began to read.

Dear Katie,
I hope this letter finds you well. We are settled in Kansas. Beatrice finds it too hot and dusty here in the summer.

I have been asked by my bishop and by Bishop Zook to seek a mending between us. Bishop Zook has written to tell me you have a daughter named Rachel, for our mother. When I heard this I knew God had chosen this time for me to reveal the truth to you, Katie. Rachel was not your mother's name.

Katie stared at the words in shock. What

did he mean? Fearfully, she continued reading.

Our family farm was in the hill country of Belize. A young native woman, an orphan named Lucita, worked for us. She was much loved by my mother. One day she came to my mother to confess she was pregnant. She did not want the child. She asked my mother to take you and raise you. We never learned who your father was. Lucita died when you were born and my mother took you in as Lucita had wished and raised you as her own.

Because my father was dead, speculation began to circulate in the church that the child was Mother's. Such gossip caused her great distress. She denied it, but some women who did not like her kept the gossip alive. The bishop asked Mother to repent, she refused and was shunned. It finally drove us to leave.

Katie laid the letter down without reading more. Her mind reeled. She wanted to pinch herself and wake from this bad dream. No wonder she'd never felt as if she fit in. She wasn't a Lantz. She wasn't Amish. Her black hair and eyes were a gift from a

245

mother she'd never known. She stared at the grass littered with apple blossoms in front of her without seeing it. After a few minutes, she began reading again.

I did not wish to leave Belize. There was someone I planned to marry there, but as father was dead, I was the head of the house. It was my responsibility to take care of my mother and the rest of the family. When everyone died in that fire, I could not look upon your face without seeing all I had lost because of you.

Perhaps I was too hard on you when you were growing up. If I was, it was because I saw your mother's wildness in you and wished to stem it.

Beatrice and I have come, at last, to accept that God does not mean to bless us with children of our own. It will not be easy for you, an unwed mother, to raise a child by yourself. Please consider letting us raise her for you. We have a good home. She will not want for anything. You may see her often if you wish. I know of work nearby if you choose to move here.

As I told you the day you left, if you had come to me in person, Katie, and shown repentance, I would have taken you in. I shall now tell my bishop all is mended between us.

Malachi Lantz

Katie wadded the letter up and threw it into the grass. How dare Malachi offer to take her baby after making her miserable her entire life! Rising to her feet, she paced back and forth. Pausing to calm herself, she saw Elam watching her.

Elam asked, "What does he say?"

She wanted to run to Elam's embrace and cry out her heartache, but something held her back. "He told me the truth. Finally. Read it for yourself." She turned away instead and began walking out into the fields to be alone.

She had no family. She didn't belong anywhere.

Elam came out of the house and leaned a hip against the porch railing later that evening. Katie sat on a rocker on the front porch with Rachel in her arms. He had found the letter from her brother and read it. His heart ached for what she must be going through. He studied Katie's faraway look. "You barely touched your supper."

"I'm not hungry."

"*Mamm* has a custard pie cooling on the counter. If you'd like a slice, I can fetch one for you."

Katie smiled. "I imagine when you were a boy you brought home all manner of birds with broken wings and stray kittens."

"A few," he admitted.

"I'm fine, Elam. I don't need to eat."

"You must keep up your strength for your daughter's sake."

Kissing the baby's forehead, Katie then leaned her cheek against her child's head. "Yes, she's all I have now."

He sat down in the rocker next to her. "I'm sorry for the way Malachi delivered this news, but isn't it best to know the truth?"

"I guess you're right. I just feel so lost. All my life I wanted my family back. I hated that God took them all from me, and now I find out they weren't my family at all. My mother gave me away. I have no idea who my father is. I'm truly without any ties to this world."

"A family is more than blood, Katie. You know this. Those who live in our hearts are our family." He reached across and laid a hand on her arm.

He longed to ask her to become part of his family, to marry him, but fear held back his words. He had asked Salome to marry him and she had taken her vows to the church without meaning them. The result was that she was shunned by her family and friends for the rest of her life. He couldn't bear to have that happen to Katie.

She seemed so remote, as though she needed to separate herself from all that had gone on. Rocking back and forth, she held her baby, looking as lost and alone as she had that day at the bus station.

"It's going to be all right, Katie."

She didn't seem to hear him. He moved his hand to her cheek. "What can I do to help you?"

Pulling away, she said, "Nothing. I just want to be alone for a little while."

He stood but couldn't bring himself to leave her. "I wish you would not take this so hard."

Rising to her feet, she gave him a brave smile. "I'm not. I'm going to stop dreaming of things that can't be and make my own way in the world. It will be Rachel and me and that will be enough."

She left him and went into the house, closing the door softly behind her.

Elam sat back down in the rocker. It might be enough for her, but it would not be enough for him. He wanted to be included in their lives. He loved them both.

Katie was on the right path. When she had made her baptism and her hurts had healed, he would offer her his heart, his home and his family as her own.

His mother had told him about Katie's job and her plan to move into town. He was prepared to bide his time. Katie Lantz was a woman worth waiting for.

Kate's first day of working for Emma Wadler proved to be easier than she expected. The Wadler Inn sat at the west end of town, overlooking a valley dotted with white Amish farmsteads. The view was unspoiled by power lines, as none of the families beyond the edge of the city in that direction used electricity.

Emma's rooms were small and quaint. The beds were covered with bright Amish quilts, and the furniture had all been made by local craftsmen. Her large gathering room boasted a wide, brick fireplace and soft sofas that the tourists seemed to love.

Katie's duties were to answer the phone, to take reservations and to keep Grandma Wadler company. The latter proved to be the easiest task of all. Grandma Wadler had made it her mission in life to spoil Rachel the moment she met her.

Knowing she was lucky to find a job where she could keep Rachel with her, Katie allowed the wheelchair-bound woman to hold and rock the baby whenever Rachel was awake.

Emma's current group of guests were a family from Arizona. They were genuinely interested in learning about Amish culture. Katie was happy to answer their questions. They were disappointed to learn that they should avoid photographing the Amish, but heartily promised to drive slowly and watch out for buggies on the area's winding, narrow roads.

When five o'clock rolled around, Katie was ready to go home and put her feet up. When she walked outside with Rachel in her bassinet, Elam was waiting to take her home.

"How was it?" he asked, as she climbed in the buggy.

"It wasn't bad. Emma is very nice and her mother is easy to please."

After guiding the horse into the traffic, he settled back and took a peek at Rachel. "How did *moppel* like being a working woman?"

"She isn't a fat baby. I wish you and your mother wouldn't call her that."

"Ach, she's just plump enough to suit me."

"That's right. You don't like skinny women."

He eyed Katie up and down. "I make an occasional exception."

She felt the blood rush to her cheeks. Was he implying he found her attractive? Perhaps there was hope for her after all.

Before she could think of a comeback, he changed the subject.

"Mr. Imhoff is bringing over one of his ponies and a cart for you to use until you move into town."

"That's very kind of him."

"*Jah,* it's kind but we both know why he's doing it." Elam rolled his eyes and grinned.

Katie giggled. "To impress your mother."

"She was baking a lemon sponge cake when I left the house."

"Let me guess. It's Mr. Imhoff's favorite."

They looked at each other and both ducked their heads as they began laughing. Still smiling, Katie studied the man beside her. It felt good to laugh with him. She'd shared so many things with him that she hadn't shared with anyone else.

She loved his quiet strength, his bright eyes and ready smile. He was a good man. She was blessed to be able to call him a friend.

Content to ride beside Elam, Katie enjoyed the rest of the trip home. As Judy turned into a lane, Katie tucked the memory of her time with Elam into a special place in her heart. When she had her own place, these rides with him would stop. But until then, she would cherish their time alone.

The following day was "off" Sunday, a day of rest, but without a preaching service. It was a day normally devoted to reading the Bible and visiting among friends. Katie was reading from the German Bible and struggling a bit with the language. Elam was helping her. She was determined to finish the chapter while Rachel was napping.

"Is that a car I hear?" Nettie looked over the top of her spectacles toward the door.

Katie glanced up. "Maybe Amber has come for a visit."

Rising, Katie walked to the screen door to look out. Her heart jumped into her throat and lodged there. It wasn't Amber.

Matt stepped out of a dark blue sedan in front of the house.

CHAPTER SEVENTEEN

Shocked beyond words, Katie could only stare. What was Matt doing here?

Elam, sipping a cup of coffee, didn't bother looking up. "Amber is always welcome."

"It's not Amber." Katie didn't explain. She simply opened the door and walked outside.

Matt had changed a bit in the four months since she'd last seen him. Had it only been four months? It seemed like a lifetime.

He was still good-looking in a reckless sort of way. His long, dark hair had been cut and was neatly styled now. The diamond earring he normally wore was missing from his earlobe. His clothes were casual and expensive.

She hadn't realized until this moment how much better looking Elam was than her former boyfriend. Elam's goodness came from within. His clothes might be homemade and simple, but his heart was genuine.

Matt's face brightened when he caught sight of Katie. He held out his arms. "I found you at last."

When she didn't move, he slowly lowered his arms and slipped his hands in the pockets of his pants.

Katie found her voice at last. "What do you want, Matt?"

"What do I want? I've come to bring you home. I see your brother's got you wearing one of those sacks again."

She smoothed the front of her apron. "I chose to dress Plain, Matt. My brother had nothing to do with it."

"You're still mad at me, aren't you?" He sent an apologetic look her way, then approached.

When he was standing in front of her, he said, "I've come to say I'm sorry for the way I left you. I can explain everything, and I've come to see our baby."

Katie heard the screen door open behind her. Elam said, "Who is it, Katie?"

A big smile creased Matt's face. He held out his hand to Elam. "Hello. I'm Katie's partner, Matt Carson."

When no one said a word or took his hand, Matt let it fall. "I know my showing up like this must be something of a shock to you. Is it a boy or a girl?"

"It's a girl," Katie answered. "I named her Rachel."

Matt smiled. "I like it. Can I see her?"

Katie glanced toward Elam. Should she refuse? How could she?

Before she could form a reply, Elam stepped forward and squared off with Matt. "You are not welcome here."

Matt took a step backward. "I think that's up to Katie."

"She has nothing to say to you."

Katie laid a hand on Elam's tense arm. "I will talk to him, Elam, and then I will send him away."

His jaw tensed, she could see the muscles twitch as he held back his anger. Finally, he nodded once. "I will be in the workshop if you need me."

Elam crossed the yard with angry strides. Matt took a step forward and blew out a breath. "Wow, I thought the Amish were nonviolent."

"We are."

Matt nodded toward the house. "I'm not sure about *him.*"

"Elam would rather die than harm another human being. That doesn't mean he doesn't feel anger or annoyance. It just means he will not act on them."

"Good to know. Look, Katie, I know I have a lot to apologize for, but there is a lot you don't know. Let me explain before you kick me off the place."

She glanced toward the house where Nettie stood watching them. Katie said, "Why don't we take a walk?"

As they strolled side by side down the lane, Katie worked to keep her anger in check. Matt seemed to sense her feelings and said, "Katie, I was stupid. I shouldn't have left you when I did. I got scared. I didn't want to be a father. I'd never even told my parents about you."

"Because you were ashamed of me," she bit out.

"Like I said, I was stupid. Anyway, my folks were taking this trip to Italy. I got my dad to spring for my ticket and I joined them. They were thrilled because I hadn't seen them in almost a year. I honestly intended to tell them about you and the baby and then come back in a week."

Was he telling the truth? She found herself believing him. "So what happened?"

"My dad had a stroke the night we arrived in Rome. He lingered for another two months in the hospital, but then he died. He never even knew he was going to be a grandfather." The quiver in his voice wasn't faked. Katie could see the sorrow in his eyes.

"I'm sorry, Matt."

"I really messed up. Mom was a basket case. She'd never done anything without dad. By the time we flew the body home and arranged a funeral, you had already left the apartment."

"I was kicked out because I couldn't pay the rent . . . three weeks before our baby was due. You could have called."

"I know, I know. None of this was your fault. I messed up. I messed up big time, and I've come to ask your forgiveness."

Katie sucked in a deep breath. She had to forgive him. It was a fundamental part of being Amish. She searched her heart for God's grace and found the words she needed. "I forgive you, Matt."

Hope filled his eyes. "Do you? Do you really?"

"Yes."

Stepping forward, he took hold of her hand. "I want my mother to meet you and to meet the baby. You and I and our child are all the family she has left. She was lost without my dad, but as soon as she learned about the baby, the light came back into her eyes."

"Matt, don't do this to me." Katie pushed him away gently. "I have learned to get along without you. You didn't care enough to see that we had a place to live, or food, or medical care."

"I can keep saying I'm sorry for the rest of my life if that will help. Give me another chance, Katie. I'm begging you. We can make it work. Will you marry me?"

Shaking her head, she turned away. "It's getting late. We should get back."

"Think about it, Katie. Think about Rachel and what it will mean to her if you come with me. We can be a family."

"Please, Matt. I need some time to think."

She left him and hurried toward the barn, but she didn't go to Elam's workshop. Instead, she climbed the ladder that led to the hayloft, looking for solitude. Matt's arrival had been completely unexpected. He was asking for a second chance. He was Rachel's father. He was offering her everything Katie once thought she wanted.

Reaching the loft floor, she moved toward the dim interior at the back of the barn where bales of hay were stacked to the rafters. Dust motes drifted in lazy arcs across the bands of sunlight that streamed from the double doors at the end of the loft. Overhead, pigeons fluttered about in the rafters, disturbed by her presence.

Matt had come back for her. He had asked

for her forgiveness and she had forgiven him. Now what? He was offering her something she'd never truly had — a family. But a family away from the Amish life she had finally grown to love.

She had a choice. Go with Matt or stay near Elam. Elam, a devout man of the Plain faith. Would he be able to return her love? Would Elam trust that she had truly found her way back to God?

She heard a rustling behind her and turned to see Elam, pitchfork in hand, standing at the wide doors.

He said, "I'm sorry if I frightened you."

She smiled at him. "You could never frighten me."

He came toward her. Laying the pitchfork aside, he took a seat beside her in the hay. His hand lay close to hers but not touching. She wanted him to hold her hand. She wanted him to kiss her and wipe away this feeling of being alone.

"I saw you out walking with Matt. Will he be staying long?"

She sighed. "That depends."

"On what?"

"On me." Suddenly, she couldn't stand it any longer. She grasped his hand. "Elam, I don't know what to do."

He didn't draw her close, didn't kiss her,

didn't promise to make everything all right. Some of the hope she'd held in her heart began to fade.

"What are you doing, Katie?"

A chorus of chirping began overhead. Katie looked up to see a mother swallow returning to her mud nest in the rafters. Katie held on to Elam's hand. "I am like that swallow. I had a home here once but I couldn't stay. My life was like a long winter. I wanted someone to show me the sun."

"So you flew away."

"I never planned to come back."

"Yet like the swallow, you did return and you began to raise your young one. The swallow will nest here, but she won't stay. When the days grow short and winter comes and her little ones no longer need her — she'll fly away again. Is that what you will do, Katie?"

She turned so she could face him. "I don't know."

"Do you love Matt?" he asked quietly.

"I did. I think I did, but maybe he was just a means to an end. I felt used when he left me, but maybe I was using him, too. To escape Malachi's strictness. I'm so confused. Why couldn't it be simple?"

"It is simple, Katie."

"How can you say that?"

He looked away. "Because it is simple."

"I don't want to go, Elam. I want to stay here with you and your family."

"Do you?"

"Give me a reason to stay, Elam."

Sadness filled Elam's eyes. "Ah, Katie. Have you learned nothing?"

"I don't know what you mean."

"I wish with all my heart that I could give you a reason to stay, but I can't. The reason must come from your own heart or it won't be strong enough to withstand the trials that will come your way in life."

"I could withstand them if you were beside me."

"Only faith in God can give you that strength, Katie. I love you, but I will not use that love to bind you to a faith you have not accepted with your whole heart."

"My faith can grow." He was breaking her heart.

Leaning forward, he kissed her forehead and whispered, "I pray that it will."

Rising to his feet, he left her alone in the loft. When she was sure he was gone, she broke down and cried.

Elam walked sightlessly between the rows of ankle-high new corn. He wasn't ready to face anyone yet. He couldn't believe how close he had come to gathering Katie in his arms and telling her nothing mattered but their love.

If only it could be that simple.

Perhaps for the English it was. He wanted Katie. He wanted her in his life, wanted her to be his wife and he wanted to raise Rachel as his own child.

The temptation to race back to Katie was almost unbearable. Why had God laid this burden upon him again?

If she chose to return to the outside world with Matt, Elam didn't think he could bear it.

The Lord never gave a man more than he could bear; yet if that were true why did his heart ache like it was being torn in two? He could barely draw a breath past the pain. Tears filled his eyes and he stumbled on the rough ground. Pressing the heels of his hands to stem the flow of tears, he dropped to his knees in the rich earth.

"Why, God? Why didn't you send me a woman of my own faith to love? Why must you test me? What have I done to deserve this sorrow?"

If he had given in to the pleading in Katie's eyes and asked her to stay, how much worse would it be to lose her later?

Elam sank back onto his heels. How could

it be worse than this?

I could go with her into the English world.

Even as the tiny voice in his mind whispered the words, Elam knew he could not act upon them. He had made a vow to God and before the members of his church. If he broke that promise, what value would any promise he made in the future hold?

He tipped back his head and blinked away the tears to stare at the blue sky. "Your will be done, Lord. Give me Your strength, I beseech You."

When Katie came out of the barn, she saw Matt smoking a cigarette while leaning on the railing of the front porch. He held up the butt. "I'm trying to quit. Don't tell my mom. She thinks I already have."

Katie stared at him a long moment.

Poor Matt. He's trying to become a better man, but he's still willing to backslide and deceive others.

A passage from *Luke* 16 flashed into her mind.

He that is faithful in that which is least is faithful also in much: and he that is unjust in the least is unjust also in much.

Matt bent forward to look at her more closely. "Have you been crying?"

How can I judge him harshly when I am

264

guilty of the same thing? Forgive me, Father, for failing You in so many ways. She drew a deep breath. "I was, but I'm fine now. You should be truthful with your mother."

"You're right."

"Matt, we need to talk."

He ground the cigarette butt beneath the toe of his shoe. "That's why I'm here."

"I can't go back with you."

"Katie, I know I treated you badly, but it won't happen again. My father's death made me see things in a different light. I'm all the family my mother has. I want you and Rachel to become part of that. She's beautiful, by the way. She has your eyes and your hair. Mrs. Sutter let me hold her."

"I'm Amish, Matt." As she said the words, she knew in her heart that they were true. She was Amish. Not by blood or because of her family, but by choice.

He looked at her funny. "I know."

"That means so many different things that I don't expect you to understand it all, but one thing it means is that marriage to someone outside of my faith is forbidden."

"I thought you had to go through some kind of baptism for that to happen."

"I will be baptized in a few months."

"How can this be the life you want? It's crazy. Are you sure?"

"I'm sure. This is the Plain life. Each day I will try to make my life pleasing to God. That is what I want."

"And what about Rachel? What about my daughter? What if she doesn't want to live in the Stone Age?"

"Matt, she will be loved, cherished and accepted among the Amish."

He paused, at a loss for words, but then he said, "She'll only get an eighth-grade education."

"She'll read and speak two languages. She'll know everything there is to know about running a household, raising a happy family and running a farm or a business."

"And what if that's not enough for her? What if she wants to be a doctor or a lawyer?"

"Then she will not stay among the Plain people." She reached out to lay a hand on his face. "And she will have a father to go to who can show her a bigger, if not a better world."

"Why do you have to sound so rational?"

"Because that's the way it is. You didn't really want to marry me, did you? Let's be honest with each other."

He looked taken aback. "I came here to do just that."

"You came to appease your conscience

266

and because you wanted to offer your mother the comfort of having a grandchild. It was a good thing, but it isn't reason enough to marry me."

"So you're going to stay and marry the Amish farmer, is that it?"

"No."

He drew back, a look of confusion on his face. "I don't get it. You just said that's what you want."

"I love Elam and his family. I always wanted a loving family, but it wasn't until I met Elam that I came to understand I've always had one. I belong to the family of God. Elam helped me to see that I am Amish."

"Okay, I'm missing something. Why don't you want to marry him?"

"I do, but Elam doesn't believe that I'm staying out of my love for God. I didn't know it myself until a little while ago."

"What are you going to do?"

"I'll go to Malachi in Kansas. I can stay with him until I find a job and a place of my own."

"You'll be getting child support from me. That should make things a little easier."

"Thank you, Matt."

"It's the right thing to do. I just wish I hadn't blown my chances with you."

"You and I weren't meant to marry. We should both thank God we didn't get the chance to make each other miserable for fifty years."

"You're probably right."

"I know I'm right. Matt, I promise I will bring Rachel to visit both of you as often as I can."

He smiled for the first time since he had arrived. "That'll give us both something to look forward to. How soon will you be heading to Kansas?"

"The bus doesn't leave until tomorrow evening. I have a friend in town I can stay with until then." The memory of Elam finding her at the bus station threatened to bring on her tears again, but she fought them back. She was sure Amber would put her up for the night.

"Can I give you a lift to your friend's place?"

"That would be great." Katie glanced over her shoulder, but there was no sign of Elam. Perhaps that was for the best. In her heart, she knew they had already said their goodbyes.

Katie led Matt inside the house where she told Nettie her plans and had a tearful farewell.

CHAPTER EIGHTEEN

"They have only been gone a day and yet I can't believe how quiet the house is without them." Nettie sighed heavily at the kitchen sink.

"You said that already." Elam sipped his coffee without tasting it. Katie was gone and so was the sunshine that warmed his soul.

"I just can't get over what a difference it made having them here."

He wouldn't mourn something that was never meant to be. "We got on well enough before they came. Mary will have her babe in another month. You'll be so busy helping her you won't notice that Katie and Rachel aren't around."

If only he had some way to block out his thoughts of them. Had he been right to rebuff Katie or had he pushed her into Matt's arms?

She said she wanted a reason to stay. He could have given it to her. Setting his cup down, Elam rested his elbows on the table and raked his fingers through his hair. Why didn't he give her that reason?

She might have been content, even happy with him. With his help she might have had a chance to grow in her faith and understanding of God's will. He glanced at his mother slowly drying the supper dishes and putting them away. Her boundless energy seemed as lacking as his. Katie and Rachel had taken the life from this home.

"*Mamm,* can I ask you a question?"

"Of course." She set the last glass in the cupboard and closed the door.

"When did you first know that *Dat* had lost his faith?"

She turned around, a look of shock on her face. "Why are you asking about that now?"

"I have wondered for a long time if there were signs."

She came and sat beside him at the table. "You know that our first child died when she was only two months old. She was such a beautiful babe. It broke our hearts to lay her in the cold ground. Your father struggled mightily with his faith after her illness and death."

"It must have been terrible."

"It was *Gotte wille.* He needed her in Heaven more than we needed her here on earth, although we cannot understand why. You father never got over her loss."

"But he was a good and faithful servant all the years I was growing up."

"He went through the motions for me. There were times I almost believed he had found his way back to God, but then I would see something in his eyes and I would know he had not. I was not surprised the day he announced that he wouldn't go to the preaching anymore. He could not forgive God for taking his baby girl from him."

"Do you wish he'd gone on pretending?"

"No. I wish he could have opened his heart to God's healing power the way Katie was able to. I'm sorry it did not work out for the two of you. I thought you cared for each other."

Elam set his cup on the table. "She was only pretending or she would not have gone back to the English."

"What do you mean? She has not gone back to the English."

He looked up sharply. "She left with Matt. I saw them."

Cocking her head to the side, Nettie said, "Yes, he gave her a ride to Amber Bradley's place. She's taking the bus to her brother's. She plans to stay with him only until she can get a job. I thought you knew this."

Elam jumped to his feet. "She's taking the bus?"

"Did I not just say that?"

She hadn't left with Matt. He still had a chance. "I must get to the bus station."

"Why?"

"Because I love her. I drove her away with my false pride instead of believing she was the one God chose for me."

He snatched his hat from the peg and jammed it on his head on the way out the door.

Katie sat in the front seat of Amber's car as she drove them to the bus station. Rachel slept quietly in the infant seat in the back. "Thanks for giving me a lift."

"No problem. Are you sure you won't change your mind and stay in Hope Springs?"

It would be too painful to live in the same community with Elam. To see him at worship and at gatherings and to know he didn't trust that her faith was genuine.

"I think it's better that I go to Malachi. He will take care of us until I can manage on my own."

"I'm going to miss you and Rachel."

"We will miss you, too."

When they reached the station, Amber

carried Katie's suitcase to the pile waiting to be loaded on the bus. The two women faced each other then hugged one another fiercely. "Take care of yourself and that beautiful baby," Amber whispered.

"I will. God bless you for all you've done for us." Drawing away, Katie straightened her bonnet and picked up Rachel, now sleeping in her bassinet. She entered the bus station with tears threatening to blind her.

The same thin, bald man stood behind the counter. Katie wondered if he would remember her. She said, "I'd like to purchase a ticket to Yoder, Kansas."

He didn't glance up. "We don't have service to Yoder. The nearest town is Hutchinson, Kansas. You'll have to make connections in St. Louis and Kansas City."

"That will be fine. Is it still one hundred and sixty-nine dollars?"

He looked up at that. "Yes, it is. Do you have enough this time?"

"I do." She laid the bills on the counter.

"No, you don't," a man said behind her.

She recognized the voice instantly. It was Elam.

"I have enough." She didn't turn around. She didn't trust herself not to start crying.

"You haven't paid me for Rachel's baby

273

bed." He was right behind her. She could feel the warmth of him through the fabric of her Amish dress.

Reaching around her, he took the money from the counter. "Now you cannot leave."

"I don't have a reason to stay." Her heart was beating so hard she thought it might burst.

Quietly, he said, "God willing, I shall spend my life giving you a thousand reasons to be glad you stayed."

She turned at last to face him, the love she'd tried to hide shining in her eyes. "Malachi says it's very hot and dusty in Kansas."

Elam covered her hands with his own. She could feel him trembling. He said, "It doesn't sound like a good place for Rachel."

Behind her, the man at the counter said, "Do you want a ticket or not?"

She smiled at Elam. "It seems I can't afford one."

Elam drew a deep breath. "Come. I'll give you a ride home."

Outside, Katie climbed sedately into the buggy, although she was so happy she wanted to shout. Elam helped her in, then handed her the baby and climbed up after them. With a cluck of his tongue he sent Judy out into the street.

They rode in silence until they were past the outskirts of town. As the horse trotted briskly down the blacktop, he turned in the seat to face Katie. "I ask you to forgive me. I judged you unfairly, Katie. I pushed you away when you needed my counsel."

"I forgive you as I have been forgiven."

"Will you marry me, Katie Lantz?"

Her heart expanded with happiness and all the love she'd kept hidden came bubbling forth. "*Jah,* Elam Sutter. I will marry you — on one condition."

His smile widened. "I knew it could not be so easy. What is your condition?"

"I want Rachel to be able to visit her English family."

His grin faded. His gaze rested on the sleeping baby. "And what if she is tempted to leave us and go into the English world when she is older?"

"Then we will face that together, and we will pray that she finds God in her own way."

"This is a hard thing to ask, Katie. I love her like my own child."

"And she will love you and honor you as her father. Just as I love you and will honor you as my husband."

He was silent for a time and Katie waited, not daring to hope. The clop-clop of Judy's hooves and the jingle of her harness were the only sounds on the empty highway. At last Elam said, "And you will obey me in all things and without question."

She heard the hint of teasing in his tone and all her fear vanished. With a light heart and prayer of thanks she leaned close to him. "You will be in charge of the house. It shall be as you say."

Elam chuckled. "A man who claims he's in charge of his own home will lie about other things, too. When do you want the wedding to take place?"

"Tomorrow."

He slanted a grin her way. "Be sensible, Katie."

"If tomorrow isn't possible, then I think a fall wedding will be good. How about the first Tuesday in November?"

"Tomorrow sounds better, but November will do. It can't come soon enough to suit me."

Happier than she had ever imagined she could be, Katie linked her arm through his and looked out at the passing landscape. The once-empty fields were springing to life with new green crops. Wildflowers bloomed in the ditches and along the fencerows. Larks sang from the fenceposts and branches of the trees. Her life, once bleak and empty, was now full to overflowing.

She laid her head against Elam's strong shoulder. "It's a beautiful evening, isn't it?"

"Beautiful," he replied, happiness welling up in his voice. He wasn't looking at the countryside. He was smiling down at her.

She smiled at him. "Do you think your mother and Mr. Imhoff will see more of each other when you marry?"

"I think that's a good possibility. Mother deserves to be happy. She would like having stepgrandchildren to raise."

"Who knows, maybe there will be more than one wedding this fall in your family."

"It will be hard to keep our betrothal a secret. Do you know how much celery I'll have to plant for two weddings? The whole township will know something is going on."

"I can live with that if you can."

He nodded. "*Jah,* I can."

When they finally reached the lane, Judy turned off the highway and picked up her pace. As the farmhouse came into view, Katie thought back to the night she'd arrived.

How she had dreaded returning here. Now the farm had become something different, something it had never been before. It was a place of joy. A place where she could raise her child to know God. A place where she and her family would work together and pray together as God intended.

She said, " 'Even the sparrow has found a home, and the swallow a nest for herself, where she may have her young — a place near your altar, O Lord Almighty, my King and my God.' "

"*Psalms* 84:3, I think," Elam said quietly. At the top of the rise, he pulled the horse to a halt. Katie looked up at him, at the love shining in his eyes, and she knew she was truly blessed.

"Why are we stopping?" she asked, hoping she already knew the answer.

He drew his fingers along her jaw and cupped her cheek with his hand. "Because I've been wanting to kiss you since the first time I picked you up at the bus station."

"Then you've waited long enough. Don't waste another minute." She raised her face to him and closed her eyes.

As Elam's lips touched hers with gentleness and love Katie knew in her heart that God had truly brought her home.

Dear Reader,

Katie's Redemption is my first foray into writing a book with Amish characters. I love research, and boy did I do a lot of it as I was preparing to write this story.

The Amish culture is fascinating on many levels. Their dedication to a simple life is what many people think of when they think of the Amish. But it is their devotion to God in their everyday lives that I found to be most touching about them.

That is not to say that they are without problems. They are human beings with the same emotions, fears and joys that drive all of us. They simply face their challenges behind the high walls of a tight-knit community where individualism is not as important as conforming to a specific social structure. That makes for some wonderful conflict in stories.

I have several other books planned that will be set in the fictional town of Hope Springs, Ohio. I hope you find them enjoyable.

Blessings,
Patricia Davids

279

QUESTIONS FOR DISCUSSION

1. Katie finds herself abandoned by someone she trusted. Have you ever felt abandoned by your friends or family?

2. Nettie and Elam took Katie in out of Christian charity. When has someone offered Christian charity to you? How did you respond?

3. Katie was ill prepared to face life on her own. What fears did she face as a new mother?

4. Were Katie's choices smart ones? How do we help our young women prepare for motherhood?

5. Elam had closed off his heart after his father and fiancée left the church. Has someone close to you fallen away from God? How do you cope?

6. Nettie, while having suffered the same trials as Elam, has kept an open heart. What was the difference in how they viewed the past?

7. Katie longs for a family. When she discovers that she was adopted, how does that change her perception of what a family is?

8. Katie was able to forgive both Matt and Malachi for their past treatment of her. Have you forgiven someone who harmed you in the past? How were you changed by that forgiveness?

9. Was Elam wrong when he refused to give Katie a reason to stay among the Amish? He loved her. Why then did he refuse her?

10. Which character did you most identify with in this story? Why?

11. Have you ever visited an Amish settlement?

12. What do you find most fascinating about the Amish society?

13. What did you learn about the Amish in reading this book that you weren't aware

of before?

14. What was your favorite scene in this story? Why?

15. What aspect of Amish life would you find most difficult to take on? Why?

ABOUT THE AUTHOR

After thirty-five years as a nurse, **Patricia Davids** has hung up her stethoscope to become a full-time writer. She enjoys spending her new free time visiting her grandchildren, doing some long overdue yard work and traveling to research her story locations. She resides with her husband in Wichita, Kansas. Pat always enjoys hearing from her readers. You can visit her on the Web at www.patriciadavids.com.